NUMBER FOUR ★ GHOST TOWN MYSTERY SERIES ★ GOLD HILL, NEVADA

GHOSTOWNERS

The Haunted Horse of Gold Hill

BY CALAMITY JAN

♡ to Jenna   Calamity Jan

For information contact:

WildWest Publishing
P.O. Box 11658
Olympia, WA 98508

Cover and book design by Kathy Campbell
Cover and text photographs by Jan Pierson and Carrol Abel

Wild Horse Photography by Carrol Abel
www.wildspiritcollection.com

Second WildWest Edition, 2007

ISBN: 0-9721800-3-6
ISBN 13: 978-0-9721800-3-0
LCCN: 2005907910

http://www.calamityjan.com

*W*ith special thanks to those who have made this book possible:

Lacy J. Dalton, Founder and President of Let 'em Run

Olivia Fiamengo, former Director of
The Comstock Wild Horse & Mining Museum

Joe and Ellie Curtis, Mark Twain's Bookstore, Virginia City, Nevada

Sgt. Pedersen, Storey County Sheriff's Department,
Virginia City, Nevada

Carol and Bill Fain, Proprietors, Gold Hill Hotel, Gold Hill, Nevada

June Strovas, Diana Motsinger, Julia Wasson
and Alice Lindemuth, Editors

Robin Rodeau, who guided me to the cemetery

LeRoy All, Laurie & Jordan Schissler, Blake & Patty Pierson

Craig Downer, Wildlife Ecologist

Ken Schlichte, Washington State Dept. of Natural Resources, Retired

And special thanks to Carrol Abel, gifted Reno photographer,
whose magnificent mustang images inspired me
and gave substance and beauty to this work.

Finally

With Love and Appreciation to
Brooks, Trevor, and Soryn
Who inspire me always.

Gold Hill, Nevada

Christmas Eve, 1871.

Nine-year-old John, and his fourteen-year-old brother, Henry, hurried out into a wild Sierra Nevada blizzard to search for their missing horse. Three days later, their father found them lifeless on the mountain with the horse standing guard over them.

People still see the horse running like the wind, his arched, glistening neck catching the light of the eastern Sierra sunrise. His strong, muscled body blends with the earth, the sky, the wild dusty hills and canyons of the Virginia Range. Sometimes, people say, the glistening is a tear.

For over a hundred years, children and families still bring flowers and toys and gifts to the small tattered grave on the edge of Gold Hill, Nevada. Somewhere in the hills beyond, the wild horse and his offspring circle that grave. He will not leave. He cannot.

Contents

Nevada

★ Gold Hill

CHAPTER ONE

Spider Salad

Thirteen-year-old Paige Morefield knew she might die. One second she had been following the little colt, and the next, she felt herself drop and spin like a dust devil, down into the narrow black belly of the mineshaft. The scrunch of her backpack broke her fall and jarred her to her senses.

"Help! HELP!" Paige cried out, groping for footing. Dirt and rocks plummeted down into the eerie blackness below through the timber slats at her feet. How long would the wooden supports hold her? She choked on the dust and her fear, her wide brown eyes staring upward at the pinpoint of light over her head.

"Meggie!" Paige yelled. "MEGGIE," but her best friend didn't hear her. How could she? Meggie was back at their campsite in Jumbo Springs getting some carrots and a rope. She left Paige to keep track of the colt. Besides, even if Meggie were back by now, she'd never see the mineshaft or hear Paige screaming—she'd never find her. This freaky hole snuck up like a gopher trap in the sage and weeds. Meggie couldn't possibly know what happened. No one would ever hear her calls for help. It was as though a snake had swallowed her up.

Tears stung Paige's eyes. She'd forgotten to be careful, forgotten the

11

warnings of how these dangerous, hidden mines around Gold Hill, Nevada swallowed their victims like snakes. She and Meggie had been following the colt. He seemed lost. Frightened. He was probably one of the wild horses. They'd seen a small band on the bluff when they were driving toward Gold Hill with Aunt Abby the day before. Paige knew these wild mustangs were in danger. Aunt Abby told her and Meggie that people were abusing them and sometimes Mustangers rounded them up illegally and sold them on the auction block. She felt sick inside just thinking about it. Whatever had happened to this colt, he managed to avoid them—keeping just enough distance.

"Help!" Paige screamed again, but her scream disappeared like the wind that shivered the desolate sage-covered hills overhead. *I've done it again, haven't I? Again.* Her terrified thoughts stung like the sharp rocks encircling her. Pointing. Taunting. "Meggieeee!" Paige cried, furious that she could have managed to fall into another pit. *First I fall into that disgusting shaft at Nighthawk and now Gold Hill. Hello, Paige Morefield? Does it get any dumber than this?* She brushed away some stray, angry tears and drew a deep breath.

"This is terrible," she cried, wiping webs and dirt from her face, T-shirt and shorts with one hand, while trying to hold herself steady with the other. It felt like she had fallen a mile. She knew it would be just her luck to have landed directly on a nest of spiders or a rattle-snake den. Swallowing her fear, Paige stooped down and picked up her backpack, shaking it as though it was contagious or covered with creatures. The contents, including her smashed lunch, spilled out at her feet, and began slipping through the slatted platform into the darkness below. "Noooo!" she cried, grabbing for her flashlight just before it joined most of her lunch somewhere deeper down the shaft.

Knuckles whitening, she braced herself more securely and knelt down, shining the light into the eerie cavern below. Paige cringed, staring through the web-shrouded shadows. *A tunnel. Probably another mine.* She backed away. *Arghhh. Well, I'm definitely not going down into that snake pit.*

CHOLLAR MINE

Paige stood up carefully, shining her light overhead, realizing that the only way out was up. From where she stood, the shaft appeared narrow enough to work her way up. *Enough rocks sticking out to get my footing—maybe roots to grab. Okay, yes,* she said with firm resolve, *I think I can do it.* But her hopes fell when the flashlight beam exposed wide gaps that would make the upward passage impossible. Her short, dark hair fell into her eyes brimming with fear, brimming with tears that wanted to fall. *I have to get out of this death pit. I just have to. It's not my time to die.*

Her mind reeled with the knowing. She wasn't ready to turn into a pile of bones like so many miners before her. *I just want out. OUT!*

Oh, why didn't Meggie and I take the little train and go into Virginia City like Aunt Abby suggested? She gave us a bunch of tickets. We could be having a milkshake in some ice cream parlor instead of me eating spider salad down here in this disgusting mine.

Spiders? The thought gave her the creeps. *Well, I won't eat spiders or bats. I won't. I'll die first,* she said between clenched teeth, kneeling down carefully and shining the light below where she could see her favorite chocolate chip cookies and sandwich that had crumbled and spread all over the mine floor beneath her. Balancing on the wooden support timbers, she stared at the larger mine tunnel below. A sudden rush of hope filled her. *Could this be the main tunnel?* she wondered. Snakes or not, maybe it was her only way out. *Whoa, okay. Why not?* Paige knelt back down, groping around and searching for some way down. She struggled, trying to force one of the planks aside. Sweat crawled down her back as she pulled and worked. *If those miners were trying to seal off this tunnel, they sure knew what they were doing.*

Suddenly, Paige stopped. She remembered Aunt Abby's warning.

"Old mines are death traps," Meggie's aunt told them as they were driving toward the campsite near Gold Hill. "You never know when you'll hit a deadly gas pocket or unstable ground, or a flood of scalding water. Never, *ever* go into a mine; and if you fall in, get out the way you came in. Under no circumstances are you to explore deeper into a mine. Not ever. Remember, the way out is up, not down."

Paige gritted her teeth and stood up slowly, brushing her short, dark hair from her wide eyes. Aunt Abby was a consulting archaeologist and was an expert on ghost towns and mines. Paige realized she had better not try it or she might not make it out alive. From where she stood, she could at least see the late afternoon sky. She had to get out the way she came in, she realized now, gazing up at the pinpoint of light. Suddenly, a shadow covered the light. She froze, nearly dropping her flashlight. *Someone or something is up there.* "Help! I'm down here! Help me! Help me! Meggie! Meggie! Is that you?" she screamed at the top of her lungs.

Silence—then the shadow was gone.

"Meggieeeee!"

Paige caught her breath, realizing it was probably too soon for Meggie to have returned. But what was it? *Just a cloud covering the sun? Or some tumbleweed rolling across the mineshaft?* Discouraged, she flicked out her flashlight in the darkness and waited. She knew she needed to save the batteries. She might need it tonight. *Tonight?* The thought sent chills crawling like maggots down her back. *Tonight. Down here. Alone.*

She braced herself and tried to think straight. *Whoa. Okay, wait a minute. If somebody was walking around up there, would they hear me? Maybe. If I can just work my way up closer to the surface, they'd hear for sure, wouldn't they? The tunnel might even act like a loudspeaker. Yes!* Paige's hopes rose. She dropped her pack and began to inch her way up, digging her hands and feet into the earth and rock encircling her. Up, up, up she moved, grimacing and sweating, grabbing roots and rocks to keep her from falling. "Meggie?" she yelled again, jamming her sneakers hard against the wall, "Meggie, is that you? I'm down here!"

How long could she hold on? The tunnel began to widen and there was nothing to grab, no rock shelf to stand on—nothing. Angry tears filled her eyes. "I can't make it. I can't go any farther, Meggie!" Paige hated this. Hated being so scared. Hated knowing she might die. Back home at Trout Lake, everyone thought she was the bravest kid

15

in school. *Yeah. They should see me now. Sawed-off Wimp of the West. PeeWee Paige Morefield does it again.*

Now the tears came, big time. Dirt and rocks falling, she dropped back down onto the planks and let everything come. Trapped in a forgotten mineshaft, Paige Morefield realized there was no way out. She sat in the darkness and cried until there were no tears left.

CHAPTER TWO
⮞ Creatures of Darkness ⮜

Time dragged like a broken-down buckboard. Paige saw the shadow again a few more times, but she couldn't scream anymore. Her screams fell into the darkness below and lay there like dead things. The shadow overhead was probably nothing more than a cloud covering the sun now and then. She'd die here like the miners before her, wouldn't she? Maybe someday they'd find her bones and bury her up in one of the old cemeteries around Gold Hill or Virginia City. Ghost town vacation gone bad. Maybe Meggie and Paige's mom and dad would come and stand over her grave and feel sad. Leave some flowers or a gift, maybe. Maybe her dad would feel sorry that he'd left her and Mom and wish he'd done everything different.

Suddenly, Paige's gruesome thoughts shifted. Noises. Weird crackling, shuffling noises coming from below. She froze, then gripped her flashlight and crouched down, shining the light through the timber slats into the creepy darkness. The noises stopped.

She swallowed the lump stuck like a rock in her throat, beaming her light around. What—or *who*—was it? she thought grimly, backing away.

Shadows and cobwebs hung like ragged curtains in the rock and earth tunnel miners had dug or blasted more than a hundred years before. Now the gold and silver were gone, and all that remained were some old, rusty buckets and tools scattered around. *No bones, though,* she said silently, thankful, at least, for that. She wasn't in any condition to handle a skull smiling up at her. *But the noises? What were those weird noises? Bats, maybe? Or rats?* Paige cringed. Maybe she'd never know, because it was definite she wasn't going down into that hole and find out. Definite.

Paige shifted position and sat back up, leaning against the earthen wall once more.

Wiping the sweat from her face, she stared back up at the pinpoint of light overhead. Soon it would be getting dark and the light would fade to blackness. *What would she do then?* she wondered, rubbing her aching neck. *Sleep sitting up?* Suddenly the hole darkened. A shadow appeared overhead again, but this time the shadow hovered. Not like before.

"Meggieeee!" Paige leapt up and screamed, not realizing she had any screams left in her throat, not realizing she had any hope left in her heart. "Meggie! Meggie!"

"Paige!" came the faint reply. "Paige, you dweeb! Is that you?"

Paige almost fainted with joy. "Yes! YES!" she screamed again. "Where have you been?"

Silence. Everything was going to be okay. Paige felt like she was going to flat out explode with happiness. Yes! Her best friend was probably on her way to get help, find a rope, call 911. Something. There were no words to express how she felt right then. None. She sat back down on the timbers and heaved a huge sigh of relief and waited.

And waited.

Suddenly the noises from below returned. Odd little rattling noises. *Oh no. Not again.* Paige swallowed the lump in her throat. *Meggie!* she screamed silently. Get back here, Meggie!

Fortunately, Paige was still alive when a knotted rope began its journey downward into the mineshaft. Overcome with relief, she grabbed it, securing her feet on the knot. "Okay…PULL!" Paige hollered, securing her backpack over her shoulders and clinging the lifeline. The rope jerked and dragged until finally she reached the top. It felt like forever.

"Oh my gosh!" Paige exploded, crawling up into the hot sand and prickly sage. She jumped up and threw out her arms toward the sky and hills. "Oh, hello World! Hello, Meggie!"

Meggie Bryson's blue eyes widened with shock.

Paige stopped, her short, cobwebby tangle of hair flying in her face. "What's wrong?"

"Is it really you?" Meggie started laughing.

Paige stared down at her scratched, filthy arms and legs, her ripped, dirty T-shirt and shorts. Even her backpack was a disaster. "Well, hey—I'm still alive."

Meggie muffled her laughter and began to uncurl the rescue rope from the scrubby juniper tree where she'd knotted and drug Paige up like a sling load of ore.

Paige noticed that Meggie's face and arms were dripping with sweat and dust. "Yeah, well thanks, by the way. Very cool, using the rope like that. You saved my life."

"No, I didn't."

"You didn't?"

"No. It was the little colt."

"Huh?"

"After I got my backpack and returned to these hills, I couldn't find

19

you," Meggie told her. "But I saw the colt. That little thing kept circling right over this mine. Right over you."

Paige's chin dropped. "He did?" She felt her throat tighten. "Whoa! I–I thought the shadows were clouds. You mean it was the colt? Oh, Meggie!" Turning quickly, she gazed around at the sage-covered hills encircling them. "But where is he now?"

"He ran off," her friend told her, pointing over a ridge. "I had to use the rope on you instead of the colt."

Paige caught her breath and faced Meggie once more. "Sure glad you chose me."

"Yeah, me too. Well, here—have a carrot. You might as well enjoy it since the colt is long gone." She sat down and handed her a carrot.

"Kind of sad," Paige sat down beside her.

"I know."

"The colt might not make it, Meggie. Cougars. Coyotes…"

"Mustangers," Meggie added, biting her lip.

Paige shook her head, feeling her anger rise slowly. How could anybody break the law and sell those beautiful horses on the auction block? "Sometimes those mustangs end up being turned into dog food, Meggie."

"I know."

They sat in silence for a few minutes, thinking about the colt and everything that had happened on the first day of their ghost town vacation. "I need a bath," Paige said finally.

"Uh, yes. Definitely yes."

Paige frowned and stood up, holding out her scratched, dirt-covered arms. "Pretty gross, huh?"

"Worse than gross."

"I'd rather look for the colt, but maybe we'd better go back to camp and clean up."

"Exactly, because if we don't, and my aunt sees you've fallen into another pit, we just might find ourselves heading back to Washington to pick apples for the rest of the summer." Meggie got up and stuffed the rope back into her pack.

"But we need to try and find the colt tomorrow," she said, hitching up her pack and starting back to camp. She knew Meggie was right about the mines, though. She'd had enough. This time her eyes stayed glued to the ground, watching each step.

"The colt is definitely lost, Paige. But it was too weird the way he kept circling you like that. I'll bet something happened to his mother. Maybe he's an orphan."

"Or maybe he just wandered away from the band."

Paige munched on an apple she'd rescued from her lunch. "Well, if he does survive the night and we do catch him, I wonder if they could let him go again—if he could survive after that out on the range? If they say he can't, maybe we could adopt him?" Paige went on, wiping some sweat and dust from her arms. The late afternoon sun was still hot, but she wasn't complaining. It felt a whole lot better than that creepy mine. "I hear about people adopting the wild horses all the time, except I'm pretty sure my mom wouldn't let me, since I can't even have a hamster."

"I don't think my folks would either. Besides that, there's not enough room to haul a colt back in Aunt Abby's trailer since it's jammed with all our camping gear and her archaeology stuff anyway," Meggie replied. "No, I don't think she'd let us. She's pretty cool for an adult, but I think she'd draw the line there."

21

Paige agreed. Meggie's aunt kept inviting her on ghost town trips, and Paige didn't want to mess up and bring everything to a screeching halt. Aunt Abby was a consulting archaeologist specializing in ghost towns and knew practically everything there was to know about old historic places. She was also very cool because she knew how to give them just enough facts without getting too historical.

When they reached the campsite at Jumbo Springs, they were relieved to discover Aunt Abby hadn't returned. Paige grabbed some fresh clothes and her towel from the tent, rushing down the bank to the water.

After washing up and changing clothes, Paige laid her socks, shorts, and T-shirt out on some rocks to dry. Meggie spread her beach towel on the dry grassy bank under a cottonwood tree, and Paige sat down beside her. They talked about the colt.

Aunt Abby returned just before sundown. "Hi, you two!" She stepped out of the van and walked toward them, her brownish-gray hair catching the breeze coming up the canyon. Have a good day?"

Paige choked, then sat down on a stump with a thud.

"Uh, yeah, we did," Meggie put in, knotting her T-shirt absently. "We had a lot of fun messing around these hills."

"Yeah, a lot of fun," Paige added carefully.

"Then you didn't hike over to Gold Hill and take the *Virginia & Truckee* train up to Virginia City? I gave you the tickets." She slipped off her backpack and dusted off her khaki pants and plaid shirt.

"Uh, no," Paige said, tracing her finger down the stump slowly.

"Well, maybe tomorrow. Even though they're not dead ghosts, you'll love Gold Hill and Virginia City," she went on, dumping out her supplies on the folding table they'd brought along.

"Dead what?" Paige almost fell off the stump.

Aunt Abby smiled. "Dead ghosts. That's just a term for ghost towns that actually have people living in them. A few people still live in Gold Hill, and quite a few in Virginia City. They've restored and maintained that old hotel and saloon in Gold Hill as well as the train station. But, just wait until you see those old buildings in Virginia City, especially along C Street. You'd think you were walking a hundred and fifty years back in time. That's when the Comstock mines began striking it rich with gold and silver veins. And you must tour the Chollar Mine. It's a short walk from Virginia City."

Paige grabbed Meggie's T-shirt to keep from falling off the stump again.

"Mine?" Meggie said carefully, adjusting her sunglasses. "Uh, I thought we were supposed to stay out of mines."

Her aunt turned and smiled. "You're absolutely right, Meggie. Glad you and Paige got that message. No, I'm talking about a guided tour into a safe mine—one that was very important in those days. As a matter of fact, I was there today. Chris, the proprietor, was very helpful. They have some amazing displays of miners' equipment and supplies in the mine office. I can drop you off there tomorrow if you want."

Meggie and Paige fell silent. *We only want to find that little colt,* Paige thought.

Aunt Abby began to rustle up some dinner. "I'll drop you off at the Gold Hill Hotel in the morning. You can enjoy what's left of the town, and then take the *Virginia & Truckee* up to Virginia City. Visit the mine later. You've got enough tickets for as many roundtrips as you want. Virginia City has an incredible cemetery, too."

"Oh good. We like cemeteries a lot." It was Meggie now. "We'll figure it out, Aunt Abby. You know how Ghostowners just have to go with the situation and circumstances. We follow tombstones and clues as they come."

Aunt Abby paused. She looked at Meggie, then at Paige.

Wide-eyed, Paige got up and started setting up for dinner, her motions as stiff as the plastic plates and cups that almost snapped when they landed on the folding table. *I swear. It's like she knows.*

"Be wise, little Ghostowners," Aunt Abby said, forking the hot dogs from the small pot of boiling water. "If you're not, your fate could be worse than this."

Paige felt a shiver, watching the little wieners land on the plate next to some buns and mustard. But it didn't matter. She was starved, since most of her lunch was still at the bottom of that mineshaft. At least her backpack and flashlight had survived, and one badly bruised apple, which she managed to rescue and devour.

"Paige?" Aunt Abby said once they were seated. "What happened to your arms? You're all scratched up." She leaned closer. "Why, you're a mess."

"Oh!" Paige almost choked on her hot dog. "You know me. Rollin' around these hills like a little ol' tumbleweed!"

"Knowing you, Paige, it doesn't surprise me at all." Aunt Abby reached across the table and ran a finger down one side of Paige's scratched cheek. "This little tumbleweed had better watch where she's rolling."

Meggie stifled a giggle.

"Seriously, you two. There are too many hidden mines in these hills," Aunt Abby went on. "And once you visit a real mine, you'll know what I'm saying and understand why they're so dangerous."

"Oh wow, yes! I'm definitely watching out for those, Aunt Abby,"

Paige replied with a firm nod. "You can be sure of that." She avoided Meggie's cool blue-eyed gaze and quietly finished her supper. The sun had already dropped on the western horizon, ushering in the rising winds and the huge moon creeping up the sky. Paige needed to sleep. This was probably the worst day of her life. And the best. It felt so good to be alive and back at camp. Paige knew she had the little colt to thank for that.

"I'm turning in early," Aunt Abby said once they had finished cleaning up and storing the food back in the storage trailer. "I'm finding some fascinating artifacts around Silver City for the Bureau of Mines. I might be late tomorrow, so you'll have to walk back here from the Gold Hill train station. As the falcon flies, it's shorter to cut across the hills, but even though it's a long walk, you might be wise to stay on the road and avoid any danger. Snakes. Mines. The usual. My cell phone isn't getting power up here, so if you need anything, just check in with Carol or Bill, who run the Gold Hill Hotel. They'll know where to contact me. But don't bother unless it's something serious like getting kidnapped by a Tommyknocker, okay?"

Tommyknocker? Paige gripped the portable camp table and steadied herself.

"'Night, girls. Be ready at sunup." Aunt Abby picked up her pack and supplies, climbing into the van where her sleeping bag waited. "I'll drop you off in Gold Hill in the morning."

Paige wished they could look for the colt instead. Would he survive the night? she wondered, crawling into the tent behind Meggie and zipping it securely against the rising wind gusts sweeping across the hills.

Meggie took out her contacts and placed them carefully in the plastic holder. "Nighty-night little Tumbleweed," Meggie sang, lying back on her sleeping bag.

Paige rolled over, facing Meggie. "Okay, Meggie. Little Tumbleweed is okay, but dweeb is not."

Coyotes on the distant hills wailed in the wind.

"I heard you call me a dweeb, Meggie. I may have been a hundred feet below the ground, but I swear I heard."

"You *were* a dweeb. These accidental falls into mines or abandoned wells is getting completely ridiculous."

"Do you think I wanted to fall into that hole? It was an accident. It won't happen again."

Meggie sighed and rolled over.

"Meggie?"

"Yeah?"

"There was something alive down in that mine."

"Yeah, well what'd you expect? I mean, hello? Spiders. Bats. Whatever. I'm sure glad it wasn't me, though, since I don't handle creepy crawlies well at all. Yuck."

"No, they were some kind of creatures or—things. I swear, Meggie, it was beyond creepy. Like human almost, except not."

Meggie pulled her sleeping bag up around her neck. "Maybe they were Tommyknockers," she said with a snort.

Paige swallowed hard. "Okay, spit it out, Meggie. So what are Tommyknockers?"

"Don't ask me. Aunt Abby just said we better watch out for 'em."

Oh gross. Paige pushed the Tommyknocker thoughts aside, listening to the coyotes and wind howl on and on. "Okay, so do you think the mines around here actually do have ghosts?" she asked again, feeling a chill and knowing it wasn't because of the wind. "I mean, what if those Tommyknockers are actually ghosts that live in the mines?"

"Aunt Abby doesn't believe stuff like that."

"Yeah? Well then, what are Tommyknockers?"

"I don't know what they are, but they're probably not ghosts. She says ghost towns don't have ghosts—that everything has an explanation, you just have to find it. And she usually does." Meggie buried herself like a gopher in her sleeping bag. "So goodnight, Paige," she mumbled, wondering if they shouldn't be sleeping in the van instead of this tent. "I want to sleep and you're not helping."

The coyote howled again under the shadowy moon. Paige shivered, turning her thoughts toward the colt "Poor little mustang out there all alone…"

"Be quiet, Paige."

Paige burrowed down in her sleeping bag and shut her eyes. But it was hard to sleep. In her dreams the little colt kept running toward the mine, toward the danger.

And Paige felt herself running, too.

"Come back. Be careful!"

CHAPTER THREE

⤨ Dead as a Doorknob ⤩

The next morning Paige stood with Meggie and a few passengers on the platform at the Gold Hill station, waiting for the *Virginia & Truckee* Railroad to take them to Virginia City. Even though he barn-red station with white trim was within walking distance from the Gold Hill Hotel, it seemed to Paige as though it was stuck in the middle of nowhere.

Paige watched the spiraling dust of Aunt Abby's van disappear down the road toward Silver City. If Gold Hill was supposed to be a ghost town, there sure weren't many old places left for the ghosts, she thought as she gazed around. Except for the hotel and the train station, all that remained were a few houses and some old buildings. Rickety headframes stood like tired, loyal guards over a few abandoned mines on the hills beyond. No longer were the tall timber frames hoisting ore and men and supplies in and out of the mineshafts. Empty wooden conveyors spilled down from the towers now, brown-tongued skeletons of the past. Paige stared at the remnants of mines with ore dumps and mine tailings dotting the barren sage like huge anthills and wondered about the colt. Could he survive out there alone?

"It's going to be so cool in Virginia City," Meggie broke into her

VIRGINIA & TRUCKEE RAILROAD
HEADFRAME/MINE

thoughts, motioning Paige aside from the small crowd of people that
had begun to gather.

"You think so?" Paige said absently, still scouring the hills and
thinking about the colt. "I'm getting hot already."

"Hello?"

Paige turned to Meggie.

"I'm not talking about the weather, Paige."

Paige forced her thoughts back on track. "Huh? Oh, yeah, Virginia
City. Hey, speaking of Virginia City–look! The train's coming!"

Grinding around the bend and into the station, the bright yellow
and green train blew its loud whistle and slowed to a stop. A few more
people got out of their cars and trucks, joining the small crowd of
passengers milling around on the wooden platform.

"Little Toot has come a long way, huh?" Meggie whispered, giving her friend a quick jab in the ribs with her elbow. "Guess it used

to carry passengers and important loads of freight to and from the Comstock. Now that the gold and stuff is gone, they have to settle for tourists like us."

Paige watched the small group get out of the open railroad car, and a few more from the canopy-covered car bringing up the rear. Hitching up her backpack, she climbed on board.

"Only takes about twenty minutes for this train to get us to Virginia City and that mine Aunt Abby was telling us about," Meggie said.

"I'm not interested in the mine." Paige plopped down on the wooden seat of the open car beside Meggie. In moments, the train pulled out of the station and climbed over the first hill. Paige wished they were out on those hills looking for the colt instead of listening to the tour guide talk about the sights around them.

"So, let's go see if we can find the colt tomorrow," she said to Meggie.

"Paige, by now that colt is probably in Reno. Forget the colt—at least for today, okay? Hey, Virginia City is going to be a blast."

But it wasn't. Virginia City was as dead as a doorknob. When they walked up the hill from the station and stood at the foot of C Street, they realized it was too early. "Thanks to Aunt Abby's disgusting pre-dawn schedule, nothing's open," Meggie said, adjusting her backpack.

Paige gazed up the street at the saloons, boarding houses, and shops. "Looks more like a tourist trap than a ghost town to me," she said.

"You have a bad attitude, Paige. Besides, who cares? It was a wild mining town once and, you have to admit, we're probably going to see a lot of authentic stuff." She pointed at some ancient street lamps and storefronts. An old *Virginia & Truckee* railroad car on their right looked like a museum and just up the street was The Bucket of Blood Saloon.

"I've heard about that place. Hey, Paige, we'll feel like we're back in the Gold Rush days. Why don't we kill some time and check out the mine until things open? It's not supposed to be very far from here."

Paige shrugged.

"Maybe we can learn something about mines and mining," Meggie went on, following the sign and starting down the road in the opposite direction.

"And horses?" Paige added.

"I think we need to go to the bookstore to find out about the horses. I saw a sign that said Mark Twain's Bookstore."

Paige brightened and gave two thumbs up. "All right. We'll go there when it opens. I've always wanted to meet him."

Meggie stopped and took off her sunglasses, staring at Paige.

"Meggie, Mark Twain is a very cool author. Haven't you ever read Tom Sawyer or Huckleberry Finn?"

"Excuse me? Hello, Paige?"

"Yeah?"

"Mark Twain is dead."

"Oh, that's too sad. I'm sorry we won't be able to meet him."

"Paige, Mark Twain died over a hundred years ago. The store is just named for him because he's famous and he worked for a newspaper here in Virginia City. Didn't you hear the tour guide on the train?"

"No, I was looking for the colt."

Meggie rolled her eyes heavenward and continued down the winding road.

Paige followed her and by the time they reached the mine, she noticed that people had already formed a line for the first tour. "Chollar Mine," the sign said over the tunnel. She noticed the mine office to

their right.

"Looks like only tourists hang out around here," Meggie whispered. "The only one who looks like he knows anything is the tour guide who's selling tickets."

"Except those two kids over there on the bench in front of the mine office," Paige said, nudging her. "Let's check 'em out. They look like locals. Maybe they know something."

"Yeah, maybe," Paige replied, walking over to the far end of the bench. "Hey—hi!" she said to the kid with the backward baseball cap and very cool sunglasses.

"Hi," he said, looking up.

Paige couldn't tell if the person beside him was a girl or boy because he or she was reading a huge map. "Are you guys tourists or do you live around here?" Paige went on, trying not to sound too eager.

"I'm visiting my cousin," the girl spoke as she lowered the map. "Our aunt runs the horse museum. My name's Soryn, what's yours?"

"Horse—horse—whaa?" Paige couldn't get the words out. She was stunned. Thrilled. They'd hit a gold mine right here without knowing it. "Oh, hey—cool. I'm so glad to hear that. Yes. Glad we came! Hi, Horsyn."

"Soryn." Her wide, dark eyes narrowed, her tall, slim frame stood up slowly.

Paige threw her hand across her forehead and groaned. "Oh, I am so sorry!"

"She's Paige, and I'm Meggie." Meggie came to the rescue.

Soryn shrugged and turned to the kid. "Yeah, well this is my cousin, Trevor. He lives down in Gold Hill. You guys probably drove through on your way here, huh? Are you tourists?"

"Uh, yeth—the train." Humiliated, Paige attempted to untangle her words and slow down her thoughts. "Okay, sure—I mean I suppose you know everything about the horses since your aunt runs the museum, right?"

Trevor stood up. "You've seen the horses, then?"

Meggie nodded. "Yeah, when we were driving in to Gold Hill. On the bluff. I couldn't believe it."

"Awesome, aren't they?" Soryn said, getting up and brushing her dark, silky hair from her eyes. "Got your tickets?"

"For what?" Paige asked.

"The mine. Today they're running morning tours. Usually doesn't open until after lunch. Didn't you come here to tour the Chollar mine?"

"Mine? No, I already…" Paige stopped and swallowed her words.

"No, not yet," Meggie put in, adjusting her sunglasses. "But we are fascinated with these mines and definitely want to take a tour. No, we're just killing time until Virginia City opens up."

"What about the horse museum?" Paige followed the girl toward the entrance. "Can you direct us?" she asked eagerly.

"It's on the right as you walk down the main street of Virginia City," Soryn replied. "C Street. A railroad car. Except it's not open today."

Paige stopped in her tracks. "What?" She remembered the railroad car but hadn't paid much attention.

"Ticket, please?" the man said to Paige.

"I don't have one."

"The tour starts shortly," he said. "If you want, you can step inside the mine office and purchase one."

"We'll wait," Soryn said.

CHOLLAR MINE OFFICE

Paige turned quickly to Meggie. "Shall we?"

Meggie motioned her aside. "Why now, all of a sudden?"

"The horse museum isn't open, but I think that girl might be like a walking horse museum, Meggie. Let's do it. Let's get some tickets and maybe she'll tell us all the stuff we need to know. The sooner we get this information the better. The colt is out there alone."

"Chill out, Paige. We came here to hang out in Virginia City, maybe even solve a mystery."

"Hello?" Paige shook her head, astonished.

"Yeah?"

"The colt IS our mystery to solve."

Meggie faced Paige. "The colt?"

Paige turned quickly and headed toward the mine office. "Two tickets, please," she said to the man behind the counter.

CHAPTER FOUR

⇒ Tommyknockers ⇐

Darkness grabbed Paige like a forked spike the moment she entered the Chollar mine. Her wide eyes blinked in the sudden darkness, a contrast from the bright Nevada sun just moments before.

Meggie grabbed her arm. "I don't like it in here."

"It's not exactly on my Most Wanted list, either," Paige whispered back.

"Welcome to the Chollar mine," the tour guide interrupted their words while lighting some candles. "Beginning operations in 1861, this mine unearthed the Comstock's gold and silver for 80 years."

The small group quieted down, listening intently now.

Paige blinked in the shadows of the candlelight that flickered from the forged-steel-spiked holders rammed into rocky, timbered walls surrounding them. The mine was barely tall enough for some of the adults, and she already felt as though it was beginning to close in around them. She wrapped her arms around her T-shirt, feeling an eerie chill creep down her spine, knowing Meggie felt the same. Paige watched Meggie's wide, glassy eyes flash like huge, round gold pans in the shadows. *We need to get our horse information and get out of here,* she sent a sharp, silent message to Meggie.

"These beeswax candles were the primary source of light," the guide went on, leading the group deeper into the mine. "There were fifty mines here in the Comstock, and the Chollar was just one. Believe it or not, there were 750 miles of underground tunnels, mostly all connecting. They didn't go much deeper than 2,000 feet, due to water and flooding. Watch your step now. The tracks beneath your feet were used for the ore cars the miners pushed out by hand once the blasting and timbering were finished."

Paige gazed around, looking for Soryn and Trevor. Beeswax and rail tracks were going to have to wait. Right now she needed to start asking questions about the horses. She noticed Trevor and Soryn hanging back.

"It generally took a full eight-hour day to drill and blast a five-foot tunnel, timbering it up with wooden beams, laying the rails, then mucking out onto the ore cars to the sixty stamp mill," the man went on.

"Mucking?" a tiny woman with a brisk English accent chuckled. "Rather a rude word, wouldn't you say?" She brushed aside a wayward blue-gray curl escaping from her straw hat.

"Mucking meant hauling," he replied with a smile. "It was a common term back then when your Cornish ancestors dominated these mines. Cornish miners were called Cousin Jacks and were the best because they'd learned how to mine copper, tin, slate and clay back in England. And yes—rude, harsh, hard as nails—they had to be all of that. The description fit the life of those men. It was a hard life, and many did not survive the cave-ins, deadly gases, fires, or the underground floods that drowned them in minutes." The tour guide adjusted his felt hat and went on. "They wore soft hats like the one I'm wearing. Not very protective, were they? But the Cornish miners brought the Tommyknockers, which they swore saved their lives from more than one cave-in."

Tommyknockers? Paige nearly fell over a small, rusty pail. Tools and machinery lay around like leftovers from an ancient garage sale.

"You just about tripped over one of the miner's lunch buckets," he smiled and walked up to Paige, who by now had turned blood red from embarrassment.

"Oh, excuse me," she blurted, suddenly wishing she could drop into a shaft and disappear.

The man smiled and held up the tin utensil by the handle for everyone to see. "This is a miner's lunch bucket," he said, unscrewing the lid. "On top we have the cup, and below that is the plate." Carefully he removed each layered piece, holding it up. "Beneath the plate is the tin that held their pasties. The bottom held the hot water for tea which also kept the pasties warm."

"Pasties?" Soryn asked, walking up. "Something like *Krispy Kremes?* I'm from Los Angeles and guess I haven't heard of pasties."

"Not quite," he chuckled. "A pastie is a meat and vegetable pie layered in a tasty pastry shell and wrapped in layers of brown paper. A Cornish miner's hearty meal."

By this time Paige and Meggie had dropped back. "Yeah okay, if we have to get historical, let's get back to the Tommyknockers," Paige muttered under her breath.

MINER'S LUNCH BUCKET

"Shhhh!" Meggie elbowed her.

"They fed their pasties to the Tommyknockers," he went on. "Claimed it was necessary if they wanted to stay alive."

"Who on earth are the Tommyknockers, dear?" a lively elderly woman asked.

"The little people the Cornish miners brought with them from the county of Cornwall along the Cornish coast of England."

"Why, how romantic!" she chirped. "Tell us more!"

"Silly legend is more like it," her husband snorted.

She frowned and jabbed his toe with her walking stick. "Hush your mouth, Harold."

"The legend of the Tommyknockers may have been true," the tour guide went on.

Paige and Meggie inched closer, listening intently now.

"If the miners sprinkled the pastie crumbs alongside them as they worked, the Tommyknockers stayed close, nibbling and crunching happily. They were said to have their homes deep in the underground workings of the mines. If something disappeared or candles were mysteriously blown out, the Tommyknockers were responsible. They got their names from their tapping on the timbers in the mines. During real danger, for example, if there was going to be a flood or gases were leaking, the warning knocks grew louder and the miners heeded their warning, usually getting out just in time."

"Whoa, that is amazing," Paige said, gazing around in the shadows and realizing that some of this history was pretty cool. "So, what'd they look like?"

"The miners refused to tell. Said it was bad luck," the tour guide went on, leading the way deeper into the mine and explaining what the tools and equipment lying around were used for. "The Tommyknockers weren't the only ones who gave warning signals, though. Five minutes before blasting there were six warning whistles, and one minute before–there were two long whistles. The prolonged whistle meant ALL CLEAR."

"I'd rather work at the BZ Burger Bar than down here, wouldn't you, Meggie?"

"Definitely," Meggie agreed.

"So much for the Tommyknockers," Paige told her, drawing back and waiting for Soryn. "Now I'm going for the horses."

"Cool, huh?" Trevor walked up to Paige and Meggie.

"Very cool," Paige agreed.

"Then you've done this tour before?" Meggie asked him.

"Yeah, it's sorta fun to take cousins and friends down here when they're visiting Gold Hill and Virginia City. These mines are so cool."

Paige grimaced in the shadows, then turned to Soryn. "Do you visit the horse museum much?"

"I'll tell you after the tour. It's interesting, don't you think?"

"What's interesting?" Paige said.

Soryn frowned at Paige. "The mine. Isn't that why you're down here?"

Paige felt the words back up in her throat. No, it wasn't. She'd come to learn more about the horses.

"Uh, the Tommyknockers are very interesting," Meggie replied.

"Yeah," Trevor said, "and I've seen 'em."

"You have?" Paige whirled around, crashing into a huge tool leaning against the earth and timber wall.

"Shhhh!" Soryn gestured. "We can talk later. I want to listen to that guy, okay?" She moved ahead, leaving Paige and Meggie standing by the miner's pick.

"He's seen the Tommyknockers, Meggie."

"Come on, Paige. Let's finish the tour and we can get the information from them later. And don't believe everything that kid says."

Paige felt relieved when the tour was over. She hoped this was the last mine she'd ever enter again. Ever. The morning sun felt bright and warm and good.

"Hey," Paige said to Soryn, "let's go hang out in Virginia City." Paige tossed her head casually, trying not to appear too eager. "Might be fun to find out more about those horses and the Tammyknickers—uh, I mean, Timmykackers." She swallowed her stupid words and gazed hopelessly at Meggie. "Whatever."

Soryn snickered.

"Naw, we have to go back to my place," Trevor said, putting on his sunglasses. "My folks are driving Soryn and me down to Bodie so she can see the ghost town there."

"Bodie? Bodie, California? We've been there," Meggie said to them both. "It's so cool."

"Yeah," he agreed. Anyway, summer's almost over and she's flying back home to Los Angeles in a few weeks so we're trying to show her around and do as much stuff as we can."

"Oh no…" Paige put in.

"What's wrong?" Soryn turned to Paige. "You flat-out look like you just got clobbered by a plank."

Paige tried to gather up her tangled words and thoughts. "Well, uh—the horses. What about the horses?"

"The horses? Sure. Why not visit the museum tomorrow?" Soryn suggested.

"That might be too late."

Soryn gave Paige a long, questioning look. "Too late? Too late for what?"

Meggie stepped in and laughed. "Too late for our schedule."

"Your schedule?" It was Trevor now. His wide, square jaw and backward baseball cap made him tall, almost threatening.

"Well, you see, we don't plan on coming back up here tomorrow and we'd sure like some information on the horses," Meggie continued on. "Which is how you might be able to help us."

"What do you want to know?" he asked.

"Just about survival and adopting and stuff like that," Paige said finally, trying to be casual. "Rules. The usual."

"Okay, uh—sure. Well, they run wild, and they can be adopted if they're orphaned or they've been injured. Our aunt Liv at the museum knows how to get in touch with all the right people to help make that happen. She's real cool."

"Probably a lot like our aunt Abby," Meggie put in. "She's totally fun, but also knows how to get things accomplished. We're lucky she brings us on her trips."

The horses, Meggie, Paige said silently, flashing a knife-sharp glance toward her best friend. *We can talk about our aunties later.*

"So, you're not really tourists, then?" Soryn asked.

"No, we're Ghost-towners," Meggie replied. "Our aunt brings us along on these trips because she's an archaeologist."

"Yeah, she definitely sounds like our aunt," Soryn went on.

Meggie nodded, ignoring Paige's prickly stares. "Yeah. In a way she resembles a jet-propelled moth."

Paige frowned. *Jet-propelled moth?*

"Hey, I like that," Soryn laughed. "Yeah. Kinda fuzzy soft and fun but really gets things done, huh? Too smart to hit the fan."

Meggie nodded. "Exactly."

Paige stepped in front of Meggie and spoke. "Uh, anything else?"

"About moths?"

"No, about the horses," Paige lowered her brows.

Soryn shrugged. "Just that Aunt Liv and the people up at the horse museum are trying to keep them safe and free. They're hoping to get enough support and raise enough money to give them a safe range."

"Safe?" It was Meggie now. "Safe from what?"

"Mustanging and stuff like that," Trevor put in.

"What's mustanging?"

"Capturing wild horses for profit."

"Sometimes people also let them suffer," Soryn added. "A few years ago more than thirty Comstock horses were captured and tortured to death. It was terrible."

"Like turning them into dog food and stuff?" Paige felt her angry thoughts rushing to the surface. She felt anger, but also fear for the little colt wandering alone. Helpless. Innocent. Facing danger. *We have to find him. Soon.*

"Even worse."

Soryn's words echoed in Paige's head. *Worse? How could it get any worse than that?*

"Isn't somebody going to do something?" Meggie put in.

"Yeah, the people at the Comstock Wild Horse and Mining Museum have this organization called 'Let 'em Run,' and they're trying to protect them. They're working with the VRWPA."

"What's that?"

"The Virginia Range Wildlife Protection Agency. Why not meet us at the museum in a couple of days. I can explain everything and show you around and stuff. I'll be there helping my aunt this summer so you can probably find me just about anytime." She waved and grinned.

"Okay, sure," Paige replied, backing up. "Thanks, Soryn. Hey, thanks a lot! Later you better explain those Timmykickers, though, Trevor!"

They both started laughing, then left.

Paige headed up the road, taking the fork toward the train station.

"So we scrap Virginia City today, huh?" Meggie said with a sigh. "I hear the Bucket of Blood Saloon is awesome."

"Meggie," Paige frowned, adjusting her backpack, "we have to find that colt. And soon. What if a mustanger finds it first? That is, if it hasn't already fallen into a mine."

Meggie sighed again.

Before noon they boarded the *Virginia & Truckee* train for the return trip to Gold Hill. Paige sat next to Meggie in the open car. "Move, Little Toot," she said under her breath as the clankety rattle of the rails under her feet picked up speed.

"Chill out," Meggie said, giving her a nudge.

Eyes glued on the horizon, Paige scarcely heard her friend or the tour guide who had started up his historical lecture once more. Juniper and sage dotted the high-bleached plains where skeletons of old mines and shaft houses appeared out of nowhere like wooden ghosts of the past. "The colt could be anywhere by now," she said to Meggie finally, shading her eyes from the glare of sun. "Even trapped in some mineshaft." Her words sounded hollow now. Wandering. Lost, like the helpless little creature out there alone.

Meggie pulled back her hair and knotted it in a ponytail, nodding.

Suddenly Paige gasped.

Meggie whirled around.

"Look!" she cried, pointing toward a tiny shadowed movement on the crest of a hill in the distance. "The colt! Meggie! It's the colt!"

CHAPTER FIVE
 Little Beans

Paige stiffened and grabbed Meggie's arm.

"Wow," Meggie said, as the train neared the Gold Hill station. "Okay, the colt is just beyond that mine. We'll follow him." Meggie took her binoculars out of her backpack and set her eyes on the small creature grazing in the hills beyond.

Paige gripped the wooden seat, knowing they shouldn't draw attention to themselves, or to the colt. *Meggie's right,* she realized. They had to stay cool. Very, very cool. "The binoculars, please," she said, with words as dry and crisp as summer sagebrush.

Meggie couldn't hear over the churning of the engine and tour-talk of the guide, keeping the field glasses focused on the colt. "He's moving away from the mine."

Paige grabbed the binoculars and stood up, getting a closer view of the little creature. "Oh no." She gazed around quickly to check out his location.

"We're almost at the station," Meggie told her, knowing exactly what she was thinking.

"Do you have any carrots?" she asked her.

"Carrots?" Meggie frowned.

"And a rope?"

Meggie shook her head. "I didn't think we'd need any carrots or rope in Virginia City."

"We have to get some."

"Paige, it's too far to hike back to camp. If we did that, we'd lose the colt for sure."

Paige drew a quick breath and turned to the kid sitting next to her. "Oh, hi!" she said, sitting back down and pointing to a paper bag on the floor beside him. "That your lunch?"

He nodded, bored.

"Got any carrots?" she went on.

"Yeah. Mom always puts in carrots."

"Uh, want to trade some carrots for two Snickers and some cookies?"

The kid brightened and said the trade might be a great idea. In moments he pulled out a plastic bag filled with veggies. "Keep the celery, too," he said. "If you're lucky you might even find some broccoli."

Paige almost fainted with joy. "Oh, yes. Thank you. Thank you very much." Her hands trembled as they exchanged their food.

The kid looked at her like she was a complete wacko and shrugged.

It was a miracle. Sacrificing her mom's chocolate chip cookies and two Snickers bars for this treasure was a pure miracle. She stood back up and gave Meggie a quick jab in the ribs.

Meggie lowered the binoculars and frowned.

"Will you get a look at this?" Paige said under her breath, holding up the carrots and veggies like it was a bag of gold nuggets fresh from some mine.

Meggie sat down with a thud. "Where…"

Paige pointed to the kid with chocolate running down his chin.

"Oh yes. Very sweet. Very wise," Meggie mouthed the words over the churning, grinding train as it rounded the bend and chugged into the Gold Hill station.

The passengers poured out.

"Now for some rope," Paige stepped off onto the platform and gazed around. Hitching up her backpack, she hurried around the back of the building, where she found lumber and equipment scattered around. Rooting around like a ground squirrel, she discovered some rope coiled around an old barrel. Unwinding it quickly, she turned to Meggie who stood with the binoculars still trying to catch sight of the colt. "We'll bring it back," she told her.

"What? The colt or the rope?" Meggie asked.

"Both, I hope," Paige replied, placing the coiled rope around her neck.

Zigzagging like jackrabbits through the dry sage and weeds, they climbed toward the ridge where they had seen the colt from the train. Unless the wind kicked up, Paige realized it was going to be another hot summer day here in the high Nevada range.

"You're very smart," Meggie said to Paige whose dark eyes peered out like round gold pans from behind the coiled rope necklace. "Funny looking, but smart."

"Without me, you're nothing." Paige tossed a string of hair from her sweat-streaked face, then moved on up toward the crest of the hill.

Meggie stopped. "You're right," she said.

Paige paused and turned back.

"We need each other," Meggie said. "Ghostowners are like that. They have to stick together. Help each other out."

Paige nodded and walked up to Meggie, placing the coil of rope around her neck. "You're right," she said. "That little colt needs us, too. Let's find him before some mustangers or a mountain lion does."

"Hey," Meggie paused for a moment, staring down at her funky rope necklace.

Paige grinned and hurried up the rise, sure-footed sneakers skirting the prickly scrub. Before long, they reached the ridge.

"Whoa! There he is!" Paige said quietly, crouching quickly behind some scrub juniper.

Meggie's tall, lanky frame grew rigid. She gripped the rope around her neck like it was going to keep her from falling, and then knelt beside her friend. Her wide blue eyes focused on the horizon.

"He's hanging out around that old mine," Paige went on, pointing to the crumbling wooden headframe standing guard over the shaft like an ancient wooden witch with a pointed hat. "That's dangerous."

"Maybe he likes mines," Meggie replied absently.

"Well, I sure hope he likes carrots," Paige leaned over and slipped off her pack, searching for the bag of veggies.

"Wait, now he's moving behind the shaft house," Meggie said. "This is our chance. Let's go."

Quickly and quietly they skirted scrub and sage, moving carefully toward the abandoned mine. Gusty winds and loose, rattling boards camouflaged their footsteps as they crept around the building, side-stepping ore deposits and rusty equipment.

"Ohhh! He's beautiful!" Paige whispered, catching her breath and getting her first close-up view of the small, brown creature with his black mane spiking in the wind. By this time, the colt had settled down in the dry grass. Small, white, bean-sized spots on its haunches

LITTLE BEANS

glistened in the sun.

The carrots trembled in Paige's outstretched hand as she and Meggie moved out from the side of the building. "Hello, Little Beans," she said softly watching the sturdy muscled legs quiver, then get up slowly. "Here. A nice carrot…"

The colt arched his neck, then bolted, mane and tail flying.

"Oh no!" Meggie cried, gripping the rope that she had knotted and prepared so carefully.

Paige started running. "We follow him, Meggie!" she called back. "We've come too close now. Hurry!"

The small, sure-footed creature ran like a gusting, erratic wind.

"We can't lose him! We can't!" Paige shoved the carrots into the pocket of her shorts, keeping her gaze locked on the horizon where the colt galloped up the hill toward another ridge.

"Watch your step!" Meggie kept pace beside her now. "One mineshaft per ghost town is the law!"

"What law?"

"Ghostowner's Law."

"That's dumb, Meggie. We haven't set up any laws!"

"Then it's about time we did."

"Later. First we find that colt!" Paige threw her hair from her eyes, watching the colt disappear over the ridge. *Oh please, Little Beans— please let us help you!*

The early afternoon sun beat hot. They climbed the crest of the hill, hoping they wouldn't lose sight of the colt. When they reached the ridge, they gazed down, watching him disappear into a small box canyon below. Paige's heart throbbed with hope. *A box canyon. Okay. So far, so good.*

Meggie had already moved ahead, the rope tight in her hand, stepping carefully and easing downward toward the canyon. By now, the colt had already disappeared from view.

Paige stopped and drew a deep breath, wiping the sweat from her face and arms. Reaching into her pocket, she pulled out the carrots and veggies. Meggie stood beside her, slowly unwinding the rope. Could Meggie get close enough to loop the rope around his neck? Paige wondered. *Maybe we're not doing this right.* A hawk circled like a vulture over their heads and she shivered.

Paige moved slowly, quietly down the ravine with Meggie following.

"Stop, Paige," Meggie whispered. "I hear something."

"The wind."

"No, Paige. Listen."

Paige stopped and cupped her ear, straining to hear. "Whoa!" Meggie was right. Weird sounds were coming from the canyon. "It sounds like animals," she said, her pulse pounding like thunder. *Well, why not?* "Sheep and cows run loose on these ranges."

Meggie moved ahead, motioning for her to stop talking.

Yes, animals. It does sound like animals, she realized as they drew closer. *Maybe a little farm down here? A corral? Maybe the colt is returning home?* Paige remembered hearing about "leppys," the colts who got left behind after the roundups. A rising hope welled up in her throat. "Yes, maybe that's it. The little colt might be finding its way back home."

"Shhh!" Meggie gestured again.

They moved slowly down the ravine and around the bend. And then she saw them. Horses—maybe forty or fifty sweaty horses crammed behind a gate with the little colt pacing, as though he was trying to find his way in.

"Whoa!" Paige threw her hand against her mouth, watching a shadow slide out from behind a huge boulder near the iron barricade. Meggie grabbed her arm, nearly knocking her over.

A stocky, gray-eyed teenager in a ratty cowboy hat moved slowly toward them. The muscled arms held a rifle and lifted it slowly.

CHAPTER SIX
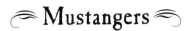
Mustangers

"Stop!" Paige screamed, nearly falling backwards. "You should never point a gun at someone like that!"

Meggie gasped.

His piercing gray eyes held them, the rifle still steady in his hand.

It's only an overgrown kid, Paige realized, bracing herself. "Put that gun down before you hurt somebody!" she ordered, walking up to the stocky guy in jeans, and a tank top. "That thing better not be loaded!"

He lowered the gun and backed up, yelling angrily. "You shouldn't be here! What're you doing, anyhow?"

"We—we're trying to rescue that little colt," Meggie said, backing up. "Paige, come'on! Let's just go back to our campsite at Jumbo Springs and leave him alone with his nice horses." She forced a smile and waved nervously. "Paige!"

"No, Meggie. Something's wrong here. Why are those horses locked up like that? Are they the wild mustangs?" she asked him. "Look at those poor things jammed like sausages in there!" Her wide, flashing eyes held his steely gaze.

Suddenly he jerked his head around and stared at a cloud of dust in the distance. "They're coming!" he yelled angrily, his straw blonde hair spiking like summer grass under his hat. "The trucks are coming and they'll kill you if they find you here!"

Paige's throat tightened, her flesh crawled. "Are you serious?"

"Dead serious."

Meggie's flesh turned the color of bone. Dead white bone. "Mustangers?" she said to the kid.

"Good a guess as any."

"Whoops." Paige threw her hand over her mouth and tried not to choke. She stared at the dust clouds in the distance.

The gray eyes darted around like sharp arrows. "Follow me!" he ordered, motioning them around the side of the canyon toward what appeared to be an old ore dump.

Paige and Meggie hurried through the maze of rock and earth to a sudden, unexpected mine shaft carved like a skull on the side of the hill. "Oh no!" Meggie skidded to a halt.

He pointed into the forbidding cave mouth that looked as if it might swallow them up forever. "Disappear!" he ordered again. "Go back as far as you can!"

"Uh—thanks, but any other suggestions?" Meggie whirled around. "Do you know how dangerous these mines are?"

"I know how dangerous THEY are, that's what I know," he cried, pointing the weapon toward the hills where the clouds of dust grew closer. "So move!" He jabbed her backpack with the butt of his rifle. "And stay quiet! Don't even breathe unless you have to!"

Paige entered the mine first, fear pulsing through her veins like a wild underground river. *This is worse than terrible. I cannot believe it. Again. I hate this.*

Meggie grabbed her backpack, nearly knocking Paige backward.

"Get your flashlight, Paige. They're not here yet. We have to see where we're going! This is the worst nightmare of my entire life!"

"Be quiet, Meggie!" Paige whispered, groping around for the flashlight.

"There are snakes and rats and spiders in mines! We could be walking through nests this very second. Oh, gross! I'm running into webs!" she cried, waving her lanky arms wildly. "Arghhhh!"

Paige's flashlight suddenly lit up the mineshaft surrounding them. She cringed, trying to hold it steady. Shadows slid like snakes on the musty, timbered walls. Step by step they moved deeper into the tunnel. Cold, dank air filled her lungs. Fear clutched her throat.

"This is far enough," Meggie said finally, cutting into her gruesome thoughts. "We'll hide behind these stupid buckets or machines or whatever they are." She waved her backpack in front of her, breaking webs and scattering creatures in a carved-out side room. "No farther. Not."

Paige shone the light further into the mine and drew a quick breath. Webs hung like curtain shrouds, giving her the creeps. "Okay. Okay, yeah," she muttered, figuring these old ore cars and crates were as good a place to hide as any.

Meggie had already backed into the timbered alcove and stood her ground. "I lost one of my contacts. I can hardly see anything." She reached for Paige's flashlight and shone it around. "This is so disgusting. I'll never find it."

"It's just as well, since we're gonna have to turn out the flashlight anyway." Paige grabbed her jacket and dusted off some crates so they could sit down.

"They're mustangers, Paige," she whispered. "Can you believe we actually found a horse-smuggling operation?"

Paige had already been thinking about it. "The little colt probably got separated from its mother. I'll bet he was hanging out there, trying to get to her."

"That is so sad. Now they'll have the colt too. Kill him maybe. Kill them all. Turn them into dog food, or…" Meggie couldn't finish.

Paige felt her eyes water up, felt the terrible truth fall like a plank on her shoulders. "Poor Little Beans. He saved my life and I can't even save his."

"Little Beans?"

Paige flicked out the flashlight and nodded in the darkness. "The colt. A cool name, don't you think? Fits. Looks like little white beans all over him, huh?" Her voice caught and she wiped a stray tear from her dusty cheek. "And so sad for the mother, too," Paige went on. "For all of them."

"Yeah," Meggie whispered. "Too sad."

"There must be at least fifty horses crammed in there."

"I know."

They sat in silence, knowing the men and trucks had probably returned by now. They had to stop talking.

"That kid is a mustanger, Paige," Meggie whispered. "But he saved us, didn't he? I mean, if they don't find us or if we don't die from a snake or tarantula bite first—he saved our lives."

"Maybe."

"What do you mean, maybe?" Meggie whirled around, almost knocking her off the crate.

"You don't think that maybe he just trapped us in here until his buddies come, do you?" Paige hated to bring it up, but the more she thought about it the more she realized it might be his plan. He seemed almost nice, if it weren't for those poor horses and the rifle. She thought his gray eyes were almost gentle.

"That scares me to death."

"I hope it isn't true, but if we hear them coming, we have to be ready to run deeper into the mine."

"Back there?" Meggie whirled around and stared into the unknown blackness. No! I won't," she said. "Mines are death traps, Paige. If we go back there, we're dead. Zip. Goodbye little Ghostowners."

"Shhhh!"

"Okay, so why would he want to trap us in here like this?" Meggie whispered.

"Because, if he let us go, he'd know we'd tell the sheriff, and he and his buddies would go to jail, maybe even prison. I mean, why not? Doesn't it make sense he was there to stand guard and look for people like us snooping around?"

"I see–what you–mean." Meggie's words were slow, deliberate. "We have a choice, then."

"Yeah."

"Stay and hope he meant to save our lives or split and hope we can outrun some rifles."

Paige shivered in the dank belly of the mine, gripping the crate until her knuckles whitened. "Yeah, Meggie."

"What do you think?"

"If we try to run, I don't think we'd stand a chance out there. We'd be like two lost rabbits. Perfect targets. They'd get us."

Meggie shivered, holding her arms tightly around her slim frame. "So we stay. And wait."

"We don't have much choice, do we?" Paige whispered. "Anyway, It's probably too late and…" She stopped mid-sentence.

"What's wrong, Paige?"

"I think I hear the trucks pulling in now. Listen!"

Meggie grabbed her arm, nodding in the shadows. "So—so if they come back here?"

"We run. Back there," she whispered, pointing deeper into the mine. Maybe we could outrun 'em or lose 'em. There are hundreds of miles of tunnels running under the Comstock, Meggie. Maybe we have to do it just this once. We haven't got anything to lose."

"Except our lives." Meggie squeezed her arm so tight Paige thought it was going to cut off her circulation. "Oh my gosh! I hear 'em!"

Fear backed up in her throat until Paige thought she was going to choke. Yes. They were here. Taking the horses, but maybe coming for Meggie and her first. She had never been so scared. Felt so helpless. And poor Little Beans. What was going to happen to him?

"I'd rather be up in Virginia City having a milkshake in The Bucket of Blood Saloon."

"Be quiet," Paige whispered. "Don't say another word. Especially something so totally stupid."

"Well, I would."

Paige bit her lip, held her fear. How long? she wondered, trying to keep her thoughts steady. *Is he hiding us, or is this a trap?*

Suddenly she heard some strange noises. Paige caught her breath, listening. Crunching, nibbling, tapping sounds. *I can't believe this. Those noises. Those same noises I heard down in that other mineshaft.*

"What are those disgusting noises?" Meggie almost knocked her off the crate once more.

"Them," Paige whispered carefully.

"Them?" Meggie's eyes flashed in the shadows. "Paige! What're you saying?"

"The Tommyknockers."

"What?" Meggie threw her hand over her mouth.

A slow chill crawled like a rat snake down Paige's neck. *Why are they here?*

"We—we don't have any pasties," Meggie grabbed her arm. "They shouldn't be here. What are they, Paige? Trevor was going to tell us."

"Shhhhh!" she cried, listening to the terrible little noises move closer. Closer. Closer.

CHAPTER SEVEN
⋑ The Note in the Night ⋐

Paige listened to her teeth rattle and blend with the noises like some ghostly concert. The odd knocking, crunching sounds faded into the nightmarish shadows as quickly as they had come. *Were they Tommyknockers?* Paige wondered. *Are we going to be safe?*

And what about the men? The trucks? Time dragged like an old mule pulling a coffin. It felt to Paige like hours.

Little Beans weighed heavy on her mind as well. Had the men taken the colt away in their trucks with the rest of the horses or had they left him to wander alone, again? A little leppy.

"I think they're gone," Meggie whispered finally, breaking into her uneasy thoughts.

Paige flicked on the flashlight and gazed around in the shadows, hoping she was right.

"Let's just go real slow, Paige," Meggie said, getting up. "Make sure. We have to get back to Gold Hill before the sun is gone or we'll never find our way back to camp."

Paige glanced at her watch. It was almost five. They had to hurry. *If those guys had planned to come and get us, they would have done it by now—wouldn't they?* She stood up in the eerie shadows, feeling unsteady on her feet, unsure. So what was going to happen to the little colt? Did they load him into one of their trucks along with the rest of the horses? Her heart felt heavy just thinking about never seeing Little Beans again.

"That kid helped us," Meggie cut into her grim thoughts. "Saved our lives."

"What?" Paige's thoughts shifted as she turned to her best friend. Okay. Yes, he had saved them. Paige felt glad, but they'd still have to report it—report him, wouldn't they? "He's still a mustanger, Meggie. If Little Beans and those horses die or get sold to someone who's gonna hurt or kill them, then that kid is just as responsible as the rest of those guys."

"I know, and it makes me sick. The whole sad thing about those innocent horses makes me sick. People slaughter and abuse them all the time and I've even heard about some government roundups that shouldn't have happened. People keep taking away their freedom. It's wrong. Something has to be done."

"I know," Paige agreed, moving carefully toward the pinprick of light that told them they were nearing the mine entrance and that it was still light outside. And if they ever made it out alive, she was going to make sure they did something to help. But would they make it? Every step in the shadows brought them closer to the truth and their escape. Or were those men just waiting for them? Waiting for them to pop out of the mine like two helpless moles?

Slowly, carefully, they moved toward the entrance, following the iron tracks that once pulled the ore out of the mine. Except for the noisy chirping of the cicadas, it was quiet. Dead quiet. "They're gone," Meggie said, blinking in the late haze of afternoon sun. It's so quiet. The mustangers and the horses are gone."

Paige scrambled up the rocky slope of the ore dump. Standing on top, she shaded her eyes and gazed across the hills. "Yeah, and it looks like Little Beans went with 'em, Meggie," she said, wiping a stray tear from her dusty cheek. "So now we have to go, too. Once that sun is gone, these hills are gonna be as black as crow soup. Come on!"

Paige slid down the ore dump and took off running beside Meggie. They zigzagged around sagebrush and juniper, sidestepping ragged crags of rock and telltale signs of old mines. Even though she felt thankful they had made it out of the mine alive, her heart weighed heavy. Little Beans and the horses might not be so lucky.

"Shouldn't we stop at the hotel and report the mustangers?" Meggie suggested as they neared the outskirts of Gold Hill. She glanced at her watch. "We can call Aunt Abby from the hotel. It's eight-thirty. She'll be worried if we're not back before dark."

"No," Paige told her, wiping her dusty, sweaty face against the backdrop of the setting sun. "It gets dark too fast once the sun gets behind those hills. Let's get back to camp and explain everything. She'll have her cell phone and we can take it from there."

They hurried toward Jumbo Springs, taking the short cut across the dusky hills.

The moon crawled up the eastern sky like a lone miner's lantern. Meggie grabbed Paige's arm. "I am definitely looking forward to my spare glasses!" she said, slowing down. "A one-eyed detective isn't cool. Don't let me fall into a mine! Arghhh."

Darkness fell by the time they reached the campsite at Jumbo Springs. "She's not here." Paige shone her flashlight around. "Maybe she got worried because we didn't show up before dark. She might be up at Gold Hill looking for us."

Meggie shrugged and gazed around, trying to catch her breath. "She probably got carried away talking to another archaeologist or something. But, maybe not. It's not like her, is it, Paige? She usually gives us a lot of freedom, but when it gets dark she turns into a parent. So, what what'll we do now?"

"I guess we can eat." Paige slipped off her pack and set it down on the camp table. "I'm not that hungry, though, are you? Anyway, she should be here any second."

Meggie flicked on the battery-powered lantern and nodded, gazing around in the pale shadows. Locust and cottonwood trees shivered in the wind. "Sure hope so. We need to report those horse thieves. Every minute counts."

Paige agreed, feeling an odd chill as she grabbed the jug of water and drank deeply. "Yeah, I wish we had a cell phone or something."

But they didn't, and even after they had finished eating some leftovers from the cooler, Aunt Abby hadn't returned.

"This just isn't like her," Paige said, feeling an odd chill crawl down her back. She slipped on her jacket. Branches over her head shivered like witch fingers against the moon. *Why isn't she here?*

"I'm beat," Meggie said. Let's leave her a note and tell her to wake us up when she gets back. Tell her it's urgent."

Paige agreed. She was tired, too. It had been a long day, a long hike.

They left the large note on the camp table, securing it on all four corners with rocks. She wouldn't miss it.

"Night, Paige," Meggie said, zipping up the tent behind them. She placed her one and only contact in its case, then turned out the lantern.

"Night, Meggie." Still in her shorts and T-shirt, Paige crawled into her sleeping bag. They had to be ready to leave at a moment's notice.

Sometime after midnight, Paige awakened. *Something's out there,* she realized, groping for Meggie.

Meggie snorted and covered her head with her sleeping bag.

"Meggie, wake up!" Paige whispered frantically, crawling over her lumpy form and peering out the plastic window. *A shadow. Someone skulking away from camp and down toward the springs.* She drew back and gasped, shaking Meggie's sleeping bag.

"Cut tha…"

"Shhh!" Paige ordered, shaking her bag again.

Meggie shot up like a porcupine, hitting her skull on the lantern overhead. "Owwww!"

Paige swallowed her fear and spoke carefully, quietly. "Somebody is—is out there."

Meggie blinked in the shadows. "Aunt Abby?" she said thickly.

"No, it's a man. I saw him move down the bank toward the water. But the van is back. It's all dark out there"

Meggie's eyes widened as she groped around for the flashlight. "We'll make a run for the van. Tell my aunt!"

"What if he's hiding behind the bushes? Waiting for us. Aunt Abby probably locked the van and you know how she snores like a chainsaw. Not even thunder wakes her up."

"At least she's safe," Meggie whispered in the shadows, pulling her bag up around her neck. "But, we're not. There's no way to lock this tent."

Paige stared at the zipper, knowing it couldn't even keep the moths out. She wished she had a club. Anything. And then she saw it. A piece of paper stuck in the zippered opening of the tent. Her heart dropped into her socks as she reached slowly for the folded paper.

"What's that?" Meggie grabbed her arm.

Paige's hands shook as she opened the folded piece of paper.

"A note?" Meggie flicked on the flashlight and held it closer.

Paige nodded.

"Read it, Paige," Meggie said, groping for her spare glasses.

Paige began to read the words, the note trembling in her hand:

> You can't tell anybody what you saw today,
> because if you do and these guys find out, I'm dead.
> I saved your lives today. Please save mine.

"That kid! It's probably that mustanger kid out there, isn't it?" Meggie said. "But wait a minute, how did he know where to find us?"

"You told him, Miss Mouth."

"I did?"

"Yeah, Meggie. Back at the canyon with the horses you said, 'Let's just go back to Jumbo Springs,' something like that."

"Ooops. So, what're we gonna do now?"

"The right thing," Paige said to her. "We have to do the right thing, Meggie."

"You mean, report it?"

"Yeah."

"What if they kill him?" Meggie switched off the flashlight.

"And what if they kill the horses? What if they kill Little Beans because we didn't do anything?" Paige said to her. "Besides we can tell the sheriff or whoever that he saved us. Nobody will kill him for that."

"Nobody except maybe those mustangers. That's what scared him. Read the note."

Paige faced her friend in the shadows. Meggie might be right. "We just have to be careful," she said finally.

"So, we go out there and start banging on the van windows and hope Aunt Abby wakes up?" Meggie peered back out the window. "Is that safe? What if he's waiting in the bushes with those men?"

Paige's mind raced. She didn't hear any trucks. Or the horses. *He's probably alone, but either way, Meggie is probably right, it isn't safe.*

"Let's just wait until Aunt Abby wakes up," Meggie went on, still whispering. "It's safer, Paige. A few hours won't make that much difference."

Maybe she was right. But would they sleep? And would they be any safer in this tent? She gazed around in the moon shadows at the thin canvas trembling in the wind. "Okay, Meggie. We wait."

"What I don't understand is, how come Aunt Abby didn't wake us when she returned?"

Meggie had a point. "Maybe she didn't see the note."

"Yeah. She probably just went right to sleep as soon as she got back. It must have been late. I didn't even hear the van, did you?"

"Meggie, you snore so loud yourself, you wouldn't have heard a herd of mustangs if they ran over our tent. Come to think of it, maybe that's why I didn't hear the van either."

Meggie frowned in the shadows.

"You're worse than your aunt."

Meggie snorted, took off her glasses, and then buried herself back down in her sleeping bag.

Paige lay in the shadows, listening to the wind and the coyotes howling in the hills beyond. She figured she probably wasn't going to sleep and as soon as Meggie began snoring, she knew it. She couldn't stop thinking about those poor horses, especially Little Beans. Where was he now? Was he jammed into the back of some truck, headed for the slaughterhouse?

Would he die before they got help?

CHAPTER EIGHT
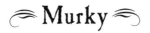 Murky

The minute the morning sun came up over the hills, Paige and Meggie burst out of the tent and raced for the van, pounding against the windows. "Wake up, Aunt Abby! Wake up!"

Meggie's aunt crawled out of her sleeping bag like a wounded groundhog, unlocking the door. "What in heaven's name is going on?" she asked hoarsely, brushing a tumble of brownish-gray curls from the scowl on her face.

"Sorry, Aunt Abby," Meggie said, crawling into the front seat beside Paige.

"Yes, well this one better be good because I came in late and I need my sleep. Good grief, it's hardly dawn. Which reminds me, I apologize for getting back so late. The van got a flat tire on a back road and I thought I'd never get back here. No spare and it's a long story. Oh my. So, what happened?"

The girls began telling the story, stumbling over words like rocks in a slippery creek.

"Didn't you find our note?" Meggie asked, opening the door of the van and glancing back at the table.

"Note? I didn't see a note."

Paige turned and stared wide-eyed at her best friend.

"It's gone," Meggie said, walking back to the table. "I'll bet anything he took it."

"Who took what?" her aunt asked.

"This kid who saved our lives," Paige told her, showing her the note he'd written and stuck into the zipper of their tent. "It gets pretty confusing, because you see, there was another note we wrote. But it's gone now."

By the end of their story, Aunt Abby had pulled on her sweats, rolled up her sleeping bag, and snapped the seats back in place. "Are you girls ready to go?"

"Go where? Can't we use your cell phone?"

"No reception up here. We'll drive over to the Gold Hill Hotel and call the sheriff from there. Did you see the trucks or the men? Can you describe anything about them?"

"Only the kid," Meggie told her. "He couldn't have been much more than sixteen, maybe older. He was blonde with gray eyes and built like a bulldozer."

The van pulled a U-turn and headed up the rough road in the direction of the

GOLD HILL HOTEL PLAQUE

68

main road into Gold Hill. "Go on," Aunt Abby prodded.

"He had a rifle," Paige told her. "Wore jeans, and his tank might have been white once. It was dusty and sweaty like everything around him. He smelled like sweat and horses."

"But he saved our lives," Meggie put in. "We have to try to help him if we can."

"We'll do the best we can, but without any identifying information on those men and the trucks, we don't have much to go on. I suppose he didn't give you his name."

"No."

In a few minutes, they pulled into the parking lot below Nevada's oldest hotel. Aunt Abby hurried around the front then up the steps, with both girls on her heels. The lobby appeared empty, so they headed toward the bookstore. A woman looked up from the desk. "Can I help you?"

"May we use your phone?" she asked.

"Of course." The woman handed her the phone.

Aunt Abby dialed 911, and in less than ten minutes, the Storey County Sheriff walked up the steps and introduced himself.

"I'm Sheriff Adam Birch," the striking young officer in the tan uniform said, shaking hands with the threesome. "So what can I do for you?"

He's too handsome to be a sheriff, Paige thought, watching him take out his logbook and begin writing. *He should be in movies instead of up here with the sagebrush and ground squirrels.* Meggie's aunt did most of the talking.

Sheriff Birch shook his head as though it was a story he'd heard a hundred times before. "Except for the description of the young man and location of the box canyon, we don't have much to go on," he told them. "But that box canyon might be the tip we need. We're probably going to have to catch them red-handed before we can prosecute. Can you give us the exact description of its location?"

Meggie turned and walked toward a back window. "Just over those hills and past an old mine with a witch hat," she said, pointing.

"After I make a few calls, we'll probably be contacting you so that you can show us the exact location," he told them, explaining that "over the hills and past an old witch hat mine" could be just about anywhere. "I'm sure it's well hidden. It's a wonder you found it."

"We find a lot of…things, sir," Paige put in, feeling a sudden rush of strength and boldness. "It's our job."

His dark eyes held her for a moment. "Your job?"

"We're ghost town detectives. Some people like to call us the Ghostowners. You call us what you want. Fact is, you're just lucky we came to Gold Hill when we did."

He paused and scratched his dark, wavy head of hair. "Why, yes. I suppose you're right."

"We're camping at Jumbo Springs," Paige added. "And you do need to stay in touch with us, sir. We want to know what happened to those poor horses. Especially the little colt."

"Colt? Sometimes they turn them loose," he told her.

Paige felt her throat tighten. *Please be safe, Little Beans. Wherever you are, be safe.*

"Of course, I'll let you know," he said. "The local brand inspector and the estray manager will be called in, but it's the State Department of Agriculture who actually prosecutes mustangers. As I said, we're probably going to have to catch them red-handed before we can prosecute."

"Please remember that the kid saved our lives," Meggie reminded him.

"Wait a minute," Paige added, digging into the pocket of her shorts and handing him the note. "He left this at our campsite after we'd gone to sleep. Must have been after midnight. You can see he's scared."

The sheriff lifted his eyebrows and read the note with dark steady eyes, then looked up and nodded. "He may have reason to be," he told them. "These men stop at nothing. They steal, even torture and kill for profit or just for fun."

"Fun?" Meggie grimaced.

"Yes," he said. "In 1998, more than thirty Comstock wild horses were tortured to death."

Paige grimaced, feeling a cold knife-like chill slide down her spine.

"We'll get on it right away and let you know if and when we have anything to go on." He reached out and shook hands with each one of them.

"Excuse me, but what does estray mean?" Paige asked, wishing he wouldn't let go of her hand. "You said it a lot of times."

"Estrays are horses that roam on private property. The Virginia Range, where these horses roam, is mostly private land. Probably the largest herd in Nevada. Gold Hill and Virginia City are close to the center of the Virginia Range."

"Where did the wild horses come from?" Meggie asked.

"Most likely the original horses are descended from those brought over by the Spanish explorers and domestic horses that were turned loose by early settlers, sometimes from wagon trains, cattle ranches, mining operations, and by people who just couldn't afford to feed them. Back in the late 1800s hay sold for as much as eight hundred dollars per ton. That was almost too much money for many folks back then. They often had to let their horses go and hope they'd survive on the range on their own."

"They did, didn't they?" Paige said to him.

He nodded. "But they're having trouble now. Most of the Virginia Range is private land. There won't be any place left for them unless somebody does something." He started toward the door. "Any other questions can be answered at the Comstock Wild Horse Museum up in Virginia City. You might want to check it out. They do a lot to help protect horses. They have a plan to help keep them safe and still stay on the range, including some adoption, population control, and sanctuary."

"We'll definitely do that," Meggie told him. "Thanks, sir. And by the way, if you need us and we're not at Jumbo Springs we'll probably be hanging out in Virginia City."

He thanked them and said goodbye.

After the sheriff drove away, Aunt Abby and the girls returned to Jumbo Springs to have a late breakfast and decide what to do next.

"We might as well spend the day in Virginia City, Paige said to Meggie. "They probably won't know anything for a while and maybe it'll help me keep from thinking about Little Beans. Poor Little…"

"Virginia City?" Aunt Abby interrupted, "That's where I thought you knuckleheads were yesterday. Good grief, if I'd known you were out in those hills with some very dangerous mustangers, I'd have been home sooner and knocked your heads together." She wiped her brow and rolled her gray-green eyes heavenward. "Virginia City? Is that a promise? Be home before dark?"

"Oh yes, Aunt Abby! A definite promith." Meggie almost choked on her cereal.

"Virginia City, Chollar Mine, cemetery," Paige added, thankful they weren't permanently grounded. "Ghostowner stuff. You know, Aunt Abby. The usual."

"Yeah, it's the 'usual' that bothers me," Aunt Abby said, narrowing her eyes.

"Well," Meggie said cheerfully, "you don't need to worry anymore. We've dug up our little mystery for this trip."

"Dug it up, yes. But you haven't solved it. That's what I find rather disturbing—so be wise and think carefully before putting your noses where they don't belong. Mustanging is a serious crime."

"Oh yes, definitely," Paige agreed. "We will keep our noses in the right places. Cemeteries, horse museums…"

"The Bucket of Blood Saloon," Meggie almost spit out the words.

Paige turned to Meggie. "That's beyond disgusting, Meggie. I don't want a milkshake in the Bucket of Blood Saloon."

"They don't have milkshakes there," Aunt Abby told them, "only slot machines. You want to try Red's for milkshakes."

"Guess I got Red's and the blood confused," Meggie said.

"Meggie, I'd like to finish my breakfast without throwing up if you don't mind."

Meggie Bryson shrugged.

After they finished breakfast and packed their lunches, Aunt Abby dropped them off in Virginia City.

"We need to try to forget the colt for awhile, Paige. Just chill out and have some fun. Explore this town, hike over to the cemetery, and maybe go back to the Chollar Mine."

"Plus the museum. I'd like to find out more about wild horses. And mustangers."

"Yeah, I can see you're forgetting the colt." Her sarcasm dripped.

"Meggie, I can't just drop Little Beans from my thoughts like that. Like pow. Bang. Goodbye Little Beans."

Meggie paused at the foot of C Street. "Yeah, I guess I know what you're saying. I can't forget that kid who could be in serious trouble, either."

"He's in serious trouble whether he's caught or not, Meggie. He shouldn't be hanging out with jerks like that—doing stuff he shouldn't be doing."

"Don't forget, he saved our lives." Meggie hitched up her pack and started up the street, passing Mark Twain's bookstore. "Hey, look," she paused, pointing inside the store. "He's in there, Paige."

"Who's in there? That kid?"

"No, Mark Twain."

"Excuse me?" Paige frowned, then walked up to the old door and peered inside. She caught her breath. There, sitting in chair and surrounded by books, was a lifelike statue of Mark Twain. Gray, bushy eyebrows framed the penetrating eyes that seemed to be looking straight at her. "Oh, uh—excuse us!" she called, staring at the frozen smile stuck like pitch beneath a gray mustache. "Yes. Very cool," she said to Meggie who was standing on the boardwalk. "We'll be back. I definitely want to talk to him."

"Who?" Meggie asked, leaning inside and looking around. "That man behind the counter?"

"No," Paige replied, "Mark."

Meggie laughed, her angular frame almost dancing along the boardwalk still remaining after a hundred years. "He won't leave."

They meandered in and out of old shops and saloons and museums, then up Millionaires' Row on B Street, where ancient Victorian homes still stood proud and elegant even after a hundred years.

"Ready for your milkshake?" Meggie asked with a grin, cutting back down to C Street and the shops.

"Nope," Paige replied. "But I am ready for the Comstock Wild Horse Museum. How about you?"

"Whatever," Meggie shrugged.

"Maybe we'll see Soryn again," Paige said, walking past the Bucket of Blood Saloon. She slowed down and stared at the antique hearse standing out in front. "That old funeral car probably used to haul away all the bodies of the guys who…"

"Excuse me, Paige? But, would you just drop the Bucket of Blood?"

Paige giggled. "Well, if I did that…"

Meggie rolled her eyes and threw up her hands, almost tripping over a kid selling antique buckets. "Geee."

Paige smiled and spotted Soryn the second they walked into the Wild Horse and Mining Museum. "Hi!" she called across the room that had been transformed from a railroad car to a museum and gift shop. Artifacts and brochures on horses and other mining items filled the room.

"Hey, hi!" Soryn replied. "How's it going?" Her dark, silky hair swayed from side to side as she walked toward them with long, slim legs.

"I'd say things have been pretty crazy," Meggie told her.

"Yeah? Well sit down and tell me about it. I'm minding the museum for a few hours and it's as dead as a tombstone around here. I've read every brochure in this place. Ten times." She threw up her hands. "Ask me any question, and I'll give you the answer. I should be an expert by now."

Paige looked at Meggie. "Shall we tell her?"

Meggie shrugged. "Why not?"

"Tell me what?" The dark eyes grew wide with curiosity as she sat down on a stool. "Hey you two, what's been going on?"

"Well, it all began when we started following this little colt," Paige said, sitting cross-legged on the floor.

"Colt?" Ah, so that's why you were super curious about horses and the museum," Soryn laughed, crossing her long legs. "So you guys saw a colt out on those hills, huh?"

Paige nodded. "We wondered if maybe he was an orphan, and wanted to catch him, so Meggie went back to the campsite to get some carrots and a rope."

"Catch him? I may not live around here, but almost everybody knows you're not supposed to do that, not even feed them. It's against the law."

"It is?" Meggie seemed surprised. "Well I guess it doesn't matter, now. We never got close enough."

"Go on. I didn't mean to interrupt. It must have been an orphan then?" Soryn asked, her interest clearly growing.

"It might be if we don't save his mother."

"Huh?" Soryn inched closer.

"We think he was trying to get to his mother," Paige told her. "We followed him to a box canyon where a bunch of mustangs were corralled and trapped."

Soryn almost fell off the stool. "Then what?"

"A kid came out from behind a big rock and stuck a rifle in our faces," Meggie said. "Not a pleasant afternoon."

"Go on!" Soryn prodded, grabbing her arm. "What happened?"

They both finished telling Soryn about how the teenager hid them in a nearby mine, and then stuck a note in the zipper of their tent that night, warning them not to tell anybody.

"Whoops! We'll have to report it!" Soryn whirled around, heading for the phone.

"We already did," Paige told her. "We spent part of the morning with the Storey County Sheriff."

Soryn stopped and turned back, drawing a deep breath. "Good. Wow—yeah. That's quite a story. Wish somebody besides me was here, but they won't be back for a couple of hours. Even Trevor. Hey, he knows everything that goes on around here. I can see if we can catch him at home. He might know something about that kid!"

"Yeah?" Meggie asked.

"I'll try calling him. Just a minute." Soryn picked up the phone and dialed his number.

"The sheriff is really cool but he didn't seem very worried about the colt," Paige said to Meggie.

"Well, hey, they have to try to catch those men first, don't they? Then rescue the horses if they can."

"Yeah. But that isn't going to find Little Beans if he got turned loose, is it?"

"I guess not," Meggie said.

"So, maybe Trevor knows something. Maybe he can help us find the colt before it's too late," she said to Meggie. Her pulse raced with hope.

CHAPTER NINE

⤛ The Contaminators ⤜

Trevor's bike skidded up to the entrance of the Comstock Wild Horse and Mining Museum fifteen minutes after Soryn's call.

Wiping his dusty, sweat-streaked face with his hat, he burst through the door like a miner who had just struck a vein of gold. "What's goin' on?" he asked, fanning himself, then slapping his cap back down on his dark head of hair.

"Don't be such a slob, Trevor," Soryn said, adjusting his cap so they could see his eyes. "Say hi to Meggie and Paige."

"Hi, Meggie and Paige. Okay, what's goin' on?"

"Mustangers," Paige said.

Trevor almost fell over his big feet. "You making this up?"

"Nope," Paige told him, starting from the beginning once more.

Trevor pulled up a chair and sat down, listening intently, sometimes asking questions.

"Do you know who that kid might be?" Soryn turned to Trevor.

"I'm not sure, but the Merk boys this side of Silver City hired a teenager to work their ranch this summer. And I wouldn't trust those Merk brothers any farther than I could throw a slime ball. Their trucks are all over these hills, roads or no roads. I've always figured they were up to no good when it came to those horses, but who could prove it?" He turned to Meggie and Paige. "What'd you say that kid looked like?"

"Not too tall, but built like a truck," Meggie said. "His hair was real blonde—blonder than mine." She drew out a lock of hair and twirled it aimlessly.

"With gray eyes and a ratty leather cowboy hat," Paige added.

"Bet that's him," Trevor said, glancing back at Soryn. "I see him riding around these hills. Just yesterday I saw him over past the Yellow Jacket mine, looking around with his binoculars. Suspicious if you ask me."

"So he has a horse? Okay, then I'll bet that's how he got the note to us last night," Paige said to Meggie.

"The horse probably belongs to the Merks," Trevor said. "Could be stolen if you want my opinion."

"The sheriff said he'd get back to us. He wants the exact location of that canyon," Meggie told them both.

"How long are you guys hanging out around here?" Trevor asked, getting up from the chair and beginning to pace.

"Maybe a week or so," Paige told him. "Depends on our Aunt. If she gets finished with her project, we might have to go sooner."

"Project?" he turned to them.

"She's a consulting archaeologist. People hire her to do ghost town research and stuff, " Meggie explained, walking over to a water cooler and taking a long drink. "We luck out because she invites us along."

"Cool."

"Let's hope she stays longer than she planned," Meggie went on, "because we need to get to the bottom of this mess. I'm thinking maybe that kid is in trouble."

"Or maybe he IS trouble like the rest of those Merk jerks," Trevor said to her. "Get real, he had a rifle in your face, didn't he?"

"Well, yeah," Meggie said.

"But he hid us and probably saved our lives, too," Paige added.

Trevor shrugged, still pacing. Thinking.

"So, what do you think, Trevor?" Soryn asked. "Should you tell the sheriff what you know about that kid?"

"Why not? You guys want to go with me?" he asked Meggie and Paige. "Maybe he'll decide he wants to see that canyon and let me go along. I'm definitely interested." His dark eyes flashed.

In a few minutes they were sitting in the sheriff's office in the Virginia City Courthouse on B Street. Trevor described the kid and explained that he might be the one working for the Merk brothers on their ranch.

Sheriff Birch got up. "Okay, if you three have time, let's drive to that canyon where you girls found the horses and met this young man with a rifle."

"Yes. We have time," Trevor almost spit out the words.

Climbing into the sheriff's rig, they drove down the grade toward Gold Hill with Paige pointing in the direction they had taken.

"I'll take some back roads, which I'm thinking they probably took as well," he replied, taking a sharp right on a gravel road shortly after they passed the Gold Hill Hotel. The vehicle took every hill and curve like a smooth, fast-moving desert creature.

"Slow down, sir. Back there, I think," Meggie told him finally, pointing at the familiar run-down mine with the witch headframe. He pulled a U-turn and switched the rig into 4-wheel drive, leaving the road now. Dust flew as they climbed the hill.

"Yes! Yes! That's it!" Meggie cried once they reached the crest. "Around the curve beyond that hill is the box canyon. I'm almost sure!" She whirled around and looked in the opposite direction.

"You're right!" Paige agreed, turning and pointing. "Over there! Okay, yes—we're close!"

The rig shimmied down the hill and around a curve. "That's it! That's the box canyon!"

The sheriff's vehicle came to a stop, dust circling like storm clouds. "Very nicely hidden," he said, shaking his head. "Neat as can be."

He stepped out and began walking around, looking for any identifying pieces of clothing or items left behind. The three kids climbed out, but he motioned them back. "No. We have some good footprints and tire tracks here that we can't contaminate. I'll take you back and then we'll get the right people out here to take evidence for the record."

Disappointed, Paige slipped back into the vehicle and glanced at Meggie. "The Contaminators," she whispered. "Maybe we should change our names from Ghostowners to Contaminators, huh?"

Meggie shrugged. "Or Terminators. We'd be famous, then."

"The Law isn't finished with us yet," Trevor said from the front seat. "Give 'em time and they'll be scratching at our door."

* * * * *

And he was right. Three days later, the sheriff showed up at Jumbo Springs with Trevor and Soryn.

"Whoa!" Paige turned to Meggie. "What's up?" They had just taken a quick swim and were drying off. She grabbed her shorts and T-shirt and slipped them on over her bathing suit.

"It was the Merk brothers' tire tracks, and more," Trevor spoke

81

first, stepping out of the vehicle with a grin stretched across his face. "I was right."

"So, they're under arrest or what?" Meggie asked, drying her long hair with a towel.

"No," Sheriff Birch," told them. "Tire tracks we got, but horses we didn't. Without more evidence, we can't hold those men. They've probably got tire tracks all over these hills."

"Then maybe they already got the horses off to some slaughter-house?" Meggie asked, anger and sadness filling her eyes.

Paige's throat caught. *Little Beans.*

"Okay, and so what about the kid?" Meggie went on. "The kid who helped us?"

Sheriff Birch paused. "There wasn't any kid. Doesn't appear they had a hired hand around."

"What?" Paige cried, nearly losing her balance.

"They did have a hired hand this summer," Trevor cut in. "I saw him more than once."

The sheriff shook his head. "Mmmm. Maybe he ran away."

"And the colt?" Paige turned to Soryn, still feeling the lump stuck like a rock-hard nugget in her throat. "Maybe it got away? Maybe somebody will find it and get it back to its mother."

"My aunt Liv will know what to do. There are agencies around here that rescue orphans and adopt them out if they can't get them back with their mother. Whatever, I'm pretty sure somebody can help us."

"Poor little horse." Paige began to pace.

"Like I said, mustangers sometimes turn the colts loose," the sheriff said to her and Meggie. "Tell me more about this young man who might have been involved."

"Uh, like you said, he probably just got away," Trevor shrugged, adjusting his baseball cap to keep the sun from his eyes.

"Yeah, whatever," Meggie said. "Guess it doesn't matter now."

"Doesn't matter?" Paige faced Meggie.

"Yeah, because what if the kid was really one of the Merk brothers and we didn't know it?" Meggie stayed cool, slipping on her sunglasses.

Paige caught her breath and glared at her best friend. *He wasn't one of them.*

"That's a possibility," the sheriff told them. "But as I recall, you described him as blonde with gray eyes, isn't that correct?"

Meggie and Paige stood under the noon sun and nodded slowly.

"The Merk brothers are curly black-headed men. Doesn't fit the description. There may have been one more person involved here and that note you gave me could prove it."

"Oh well," Paige laughed, running her fingers through her short, damp strings of hair. "You're focusing on the primary slime balls and that's what counts!"

"Yeah," Meggie added too quickly.

"Still, I want you girls to report anything unusual. He may try to contact you again."

"In my opinion, sir," Soryn put in, "he split and he's probably long gone."

"I second that," Trevor added.

"You may be right. Just keep me informed, okay?" The sheriff headed back to his rig. "You kids want a ride back to Virginia City, Gold Hill, or any stops between?"

Paige paused for a moment, then declined.

83

"Why not?" Meggie asked her.

"The colt," she said between clenched teeth.

"Sure you're not coming?" Soryn called, getting in the sheriff's car behind Trevor.

"Yeah. I mean, no, we're not coming," Meggie called. "We'll see you later though!"

"See ya!" Paige called, waving.

"So you still think the colt is still out there? " Meggie asked as soon as they had left.

"Yes," Paige said, grabbing her sneakers. "If they did turn him loose, then we have to find him, Meggie. He might die out there alone."

Meggie adjusted her sunglasses. "Shouldn't we leave that up to the people who know what they're doing? Besides, he survived so long already. Maybe he'll make it on his own now."

"We have to try to find him, Meggie. I'm not sure people know how important this is. That sheriff is very nice and very handsome, but he kept brushing off that little colt like he was a missing lizard or something."

"He's trying to get evidence on those men so he can save those kidnapped mustangs, Paige."

"I know," she said, her eyes welling up. "I'm just upset about the whole thing. The poor horses. It's probably too late for them now, isn't it? I hope one of them wasn't Little Beans' mother." She paused for a moment, feeling a tug in her heart. "That colt is special."

"I know," Meggie said, tying her sneakers.

In minutes they had secured their packs, including rope and some leftover veggies, and were heading across the hills. "I don't think we're going to catch him," Paige told her, "but if we can locate him, then at least we'll know he's alive and then one of us can get back to the museum and tell them where to find him."

Meggie agreed. "You may be right. They're really there for those horses. They seem to care."

"I know," Paige replied, "and even though Soryn and the sheriff are going to report the colt missing, I just didn't want to lose any time. Maybe the right people can't get to him for a few days. By then, it might be too late."

Meggie shrugged and kept pace with Paige who moved sure-footedly and with determination.

The sun grew hotter as they hiked over the hills, looking for the colt, while at the same time watching carefully for dangerous, hidden mines. Paige noticed the familiar mine with the witch-hat headframe hovering on a slope to their right. She paused, and stared at the ancient high pointed frame with rusting cables that no longer pulled up the loads of ore from the empty mineshaft below. Tumbleweeds crawled like sage spiders across the hot, windy landscape. Paige felt a shiver. They were retracing their steps, weren't they? Why? she wondered. Was something pulling them back to the box canyon for a reason?

Meggie reached the crest of the hill first, gazing down toward the empty corral. "Oh, my gosh!" she called, motioning excitedly to Paige. "There he is!"

Paige caught up, wiping her sweaty face. "You can't mean…?"

Meggie's throat caught. She couldn't answer.

"Little Beans!" Paige cried, throwing her hand over her mouth. "Oh, Meggie, can you believe it?"

Meggie Bryson dug out her glasses, straining to get a better look. "Unreal!"

Paige watched the little colt sniffing around the empty corral.

"He came back to the box canyon, didn't he?" Meggie's slender frame grew rigid. "Do you think he's still looking for his mother?"

"Don't ask me, but at least he's still alive," Paige cried, hair flying, dusty sneakers skidding and skirting sage and scrub. "I can't believe this!"

"Cool it, Paige. Slow down. We can't scare him!" Meggie called from behind.

Paige felt her breath come fast, felt her pulse slamming against the sweat of her shirt. *She's right. We can't lose him again. Oh, Little Beans! You're alive! You're okay!* she cried silently, slowing down.

"Yeah, I'll bet he came back for his mother!"

Paige's eyes welled with tears. *It might be too late for your mother, Little Beans. But not for you.* She and Meggie stepped carefully, nearing the base of the hill, keeping one eye on the little creature. *Keep cool, Paige. Stay low. Quiet.* She moved across the landscape toward the box canyon and the corral. The colt disappeared from view.

"Where is he?" Meggie whispered.

"Behind the rocks—the ore dump," Paige replied, sliding her pack off her shoulders and reaching for the rope. "You circle around that side, and I'll come from the box canyon. Maybe we can capture him around the entrance of that mine."

Meggie hesitated, then reached for the carrots in her backpack. "Or maybe we won't have to. Maybe he's so hungry he'll take the food." She handed some carrots to Paige.

Paige hoped she was right. "Okay. So, it's time," she said, gripping the shoulder straps of her backpack. "It's time, Meggie."

Paige moved carefully, quietly on down the side of the hill, watching Meggie from the corner of one eye and the colt, below, from the other. The small, finely chiseled head and arched neck shot up, tail and mane shivering in the hot midday wind. Had he seen them? She gripped the carrots in her hand. *Oh please, don't run, Little Beans. You're so beautiful. We only want to help you.*

Suddenly the colt reared back and disappeared behind the rocks near the opening of the mine. *No. Don't be afraid! And please don't go into that mine! It's too dangerous, Little Beans!* Paige screamed silently, signaling for Meggie to close in while she moved like a fast, sure-footed coyote down the slope. When Paige reached the bottom, she saw Meggie, but not the colt.

"Where is he?" Meggie mouthed the words.

Paige caught her breath and braced herself against some rotting timbers. *Not the mine. No. It's too dangerous.* Her thoughts raced. *Why didn't we think of that? No, please don't be in there! We didn't mean to scare you!*

Meggie crept toward the opening of the mine, groping for her flashlight.

"Stay back, Meggie! If we scared him into that mine, we can't force him back any further. It's sure death for him!"

"But I didn't see him go in there, Paige. It's like he just disappeared." She flicked on the light and shone it into the tunnel.

"We'll go back. Get help. It's what we should have done in the first place!"

"Wait a minute..." Meggie grew rigid. "I hear something."

Mine Tunnel

"Don't scare him. We'll get help!"

"No, it's not the colt. It's not!" Meggie's wide, terror-filled eyes flashed blue against the hot, sun-bleached rocks.

Paige's flesh crawled, her sweat turned cold.

"Do you hear that?" Meggie backed up, her face turning the color of a pale tombstone. "It's horrible. Moaning..."

CHAPTER TEN
Kidnapped

Paige wanted to back up and run, but something held her. It was as though some unknown force held her feet to the ground like iron weights.

"Paige!" Meggie cried.

The gruesome sound crawled out of the mine like a strangled, slithering creature. "Yeaaaaghhhh…"

Paige felt the panic rising in her throat. She couldn't move. Couldn't speak.

Meggie grabbed her arm and shook her. "Okay! Okaay! You're right. It's not the colt! Let's get out of here!"

No, it wasn't the colt. Maybe not even human. Or was it? Paige's thoughts reeled.

The gruesome moan grew louder. Louder.

"Meggie!" Paige reeled around, shaking her arm loose. "I think…"

"Get a grip, Paige."

"Listen!" Paige told her. "Listen!"

Meggie caught her breath.

"It's human," Paige said. "Somebody's crying. Listen." The desperate, frightening groaning filled the tunnel now.

"Paige. We have to get out of here," Meggie cried.

Paige grabbed Meggie's shirt, holding her back.

"Paige, maybe it's…"

"Him?" Paige spit out the words. "That mustanger kid?"

Meggie nodded.

"Yeah. I think so, too. I—I think he's in trouble."

"Or a trap?"

"No, he had that chance," Paige said to her. "I'll bet…"

"Arghhhhaaaage."

The strangled, frightening moan broke into her words. "It's almost like I hear him calling my name!"

"This scares me to death, Paige," Meggie jerked loose and backed up. "But he wouldn't know your name! How could he?"

"You probably called me by my name out when he had that rifle in our faces!"

Meggie's chin fell. "Oooops."

"I'm going in. I think it's that kid. I think he's in trouble!" Paige felt the strength surge like an underground river. She reached for Meggie's flashlight, then turned and moved toward the black mouth of the mine.

"What about the colt?" Meggie called. "Are you forgetting Little Beans?"

"No, I'm not forgetting, Meggie!" Her heart pounded with fear, yet at the same time ached with sadness. The colt was gone. *Just please; don't let him be here in this mine. He can't survive if he keeps running and falls into some bottomless pit.* She had to shut out the terrible thoughts of the helpless colt. Keep her head.

Paige moved slowly into the darkness as the nightmarish groaning grew louder. Her flashlight trembled in her hand, casting web-clouded shadows in the ancient tunnel. She heard Meggie's footsteps behind her.

"What if it's really one of those Tommyknockers luring us in?" Meggie whispered hoarsely.

"Stop it, Meggie. Just stop talking like that."

"Mmmmph arrrghh!" the sound grew louder, sending chills down her spine.

In minutes, they found him bound and gagged on the lumpy floor of the mine.

"I—might have—died!" the teenager coughed up the words the minute Paige unloosed the gag around his mouth. Meggie untied his hands bound behind his back—then his feet.

"You saved my life! Thanks. Thanks a lot!" he gasped.

"We didn't save you," Paige said, loosening the last knot.

"Huh?" He stood up on unsteady feet, leaning against a plank for support.

"The colt led us here," Meggie said to him, grabbing the flashlight and shining the flashlight deeper into the tunnel.

"The colt?" he asked, rubbing his wrists and ankles, stretching his aching limbs.

"You mean that little thing you were following the other day when you found me and the horses?"

Paige nodded. "A stray. Probably looking for its mother you guys stole."

"Who did this?" Meggie asked, shining the light around. "They're not still here, I hope?"

The kid drew a deep breath, rubbing his aching wrists. "We're safe for the moment. I'll explain."

"We think we scared the colt—forced him to run back here," Paige went on, pointing deeper into the mine. "We didn't mean to." She felt terrible. Responsible.

"The colt didn't come in here," he told her, picking up his leather hat. "I would've known."

"Oh, I'm so glad!" Relief flooded Paige's senses. "But, are you sure?"

"Positive."

"Okay, so let's get out of this dump and listen to your story," Meggie whirled around and hurried back out. "It had better be a good one, too. This freaky mine was not exactly in our latest travel plans."

The second they stepped out into the sunlight, Meggie scrambled up on some tailings of rock and ore.

"The coast looks clear," she called down, "but Little Beans is gone. Just disappeared. Again."

"Little what?" the kid asked.

"Little Beans is what Paige named the colt," Meggie said, sliding back down.

"Hey, you're all scratched up," Paige turned her thoughts to the bruised, bedraggled teenager standing beside them. "Are you okay?"

"Yeah. I guess."

"So, who are you and what happened, anyway?" Meggie asked him.

"My name is Brooks. I'm from Nebraska. I answered an ad and took this summer job working on the Merk's ranch," he told them. "I didn't know what I was getting into, and by the time I suspected things weren't right, it was too late."

"Like when they made you help them rustle up a bunch of horses, then stand guard with a gun?" Paige threw up her arms. "Excuse me, but didn't that give you a clue? They left you alone. You had a chance to escape. Why didn't you call the sheriff?"

"And get killed by those guys?"

"Did they threaten you?" Meggie asked him.

"You got my note, didn't you?"

They both nodded.

"I hid you because I knew they'd kill you, too, just like they were going to do with me," he said, hiking on. "I started making plans to split, but they knew I wasn't on their side of the corral and already had their own plans, which included letting me rot in that mine. You saved my life," he said.

Paige slowed down, then stopped. The late afternoon wind whipped against her sweaty skin and she felt an odd chill. "Well, not exactly."

He paused and faced her. "What do you mean?"

"We told you. It was the colt that saved you. We were only following him."

Brooks glanced back toward the mine, his soiled tank top rippling in the wind, his jeans soaked and stiff with sweat and sand. "Tell me exactly what happened," he said to them.

"The little colt hung out back at the mine entrance," Meggie told Brooks. "We followed him and that was when we heard you moaning, which totally freaked us out and made us forget the horse."

Paige nodded. "By the time we knew it wasn't a ghost or Tommyknocker or whatever, we realized the colt was gone. I figured we'd scared him into the mine, which was also terrible."

"How'd you know I wasn't a ghost?"

"Ghosts don't say 'Yeaaaaghhhh' or 'Arrghh,'" Paige said. "They generally say 'Whooooo.'"

"How do you know that?" Meggie frowned.

"Meggie, would you just be quiet and let me explain?"

"We have to find him," he cut in.

"Find who?" Meggie whirled around. "The ghost?"

"No, the little mustang," Brooks replied.

"Okay, yes," Paige brushed past Meggie and walked up to Brooks, motioning to him. "First, we have to go back to Virginia City so you can turn yourself in and give the sheriff the information he's been waiting for," Paige said. "Let's go."

Brooks drew back, hesitating. His gray eyes flashed with fear.

"We have to save those horses! You're the only one besides those guys who knows where they are! Besides, the sheriff doesn't have enough evidence to jail the Merk brothers," Meggie said. "You're the key that's going to lock them up."

"Maybe they're going to lock me up too," he told them, taking the lead now.

"The sheriff already knows you saved our lives. Finding you and having you testify against those men means the law should have all the evidence they need."

"I'll tell 'em everything," Brooks said, glancing back and squaring his broad shoulders. "Everything. Those guys tricked me. I really love horses. When I answered that ad in the newspaper, I just thought I was helping out on a horse ranch in Nevada for the summer." He paused, then turned to them. "I wanted to come to this place, anyhow."

"You did?"

He nodded. "Yeah. Long story. Maybe I'll have time to tell you someday. Anyway, before long I knew I wasn't helping anybody. Especially not those poor mustangs we started rounding up. I may not be from Nevada, and I may not know anything about mustanging, but I could smell a rat almost from day one."

"That little mustang led us to the box canyon where we found the horses and met you," Meggie told him.

"And before that, to a mine where I was trapped," Paige added. "I would've died down that mineshaft if it wasn't for the colt who kept circling the hole where I'd fallen in. Meggie couldn't find me but she saw the little horse. It never left me until she came."

Brooks fell silent and Paige wondered if it was because he was thinking about that colt like she was. He wasn't just some run-of-the-mill horse. This little horse was special. They all knew that by now.

"So the sheriff didn't find the horses back at the Merk ranch?" Brooks asked.

"No. The Merk brothers were as innocent as little doves swimming around in a sewer," Meggie told him.

"Well, I know a thing or two!" He threw up his hands and reeled around, facing southward. "I know exactly where they were taking them!"

"You do?" Meggie almost fell over Paige.

Paige grabbed his arm, keeping her balance. "Wh—where?"

"A livestock auction east of Fallon. I overheard them talking about it, but maybe it's too late. Maybe we can't get to them in time!"

Paige's heart fell into her shoes. "Fallon? Where's that?" she asked him. " Well, the sheriff will know. Come on! We have to try! Tell him before it's too late!"

Brooks took off running. "They tied me up, figuring I'd never tell my story," he called back, "figuring I'd just turn into a pile of bones and be forgotten."

"Well, you are the fastest bones in the West!" Paige laughed, keeping pace. "And you're definitely not going to be forgotten!"

"The sheriff didn't even know you existed. Nobody knew where you'd come from so they couldn't file a missing persons report," Meggie said as they circled the mountain and neared Virginia City.

Wind and dust spiraled up the canyon as they hurried toward the town. A few sheep and cows grazed on the hillside.

Finally, Brooks paused, staring at the town hovering under the hot shimmer of the afternoon sun. "I'd be dead if it wasn't for that colt—and for you." He dusted off his dirty jeans and tank top, then wiped the sweat from his bruised, scratched face.

Paige could tell he was getting nervous now. "This way," she said, hurrying toward the sheriff's office. "We can't lose one second. We have to try to save the horses!"

But when they reached the Courthouse, Paige realized everything had closed.

"Oh, no!" Meggie cried, whirling around. "What're we gonna do?"

Brooks froze, his tank cold against his sweat.

"We call 911!" Paige said, turning and running toward the main street. "I think I saw somebody out in front of the bookstore. We'll use their phone!"

They raced down the boardwalk on C Street and rushed into Mark Twain's Bookstore. "Call 911!" Paige yelled, blowing in like a sudden dust storm. She came to a screeching halt, crashing into Mark Twain and almost flattening his mustache.

"He can't hear you, dummy!" Meggie called.

Paige whirled around and rammed into Brooks.

"Owww!" he shook his already-bruised arm and scowled.

"Can I help you?" A woman walked out of the back room with a broom.

"Yes! Please call 911. We have to report a crime!" Paige spit out the words.

"Is she hurting you?" the woman asked Brooks who stroked his bruised arm.

"Uh, no. She just thought that dummy over there was for real."

"I did not," Paige replied with a snort.

"The phone, please?" Meggie said to the woman.

The woman walked up to the counter and dialed 911, handing the phone to Brooks who looked to her like the one having the emergency.

"My name is Brooks and I know where those stolen mustangs are," he said to dispatch. "Can you come right up to…" he hesitated, then turned to the girls.

"Mark Twain Bookstore in Virginia City," Paige leaned into the receiver. "There's been a kidnapping!"

CHAPTER ELEVEN

⤳ Tombstone Territory ⤲

The sergeant on duty stood inside the Mark Twain Bookstore listening to their story and shook his head in stunned amazement. "I'm Sergeant Peders. Are you okay?" he asked Brooks, eyeing the bruises and rope burns.

Brooks glanced toward Paige and stroked his arm. "Guess so. I'm still alive." A slow, crooked smile told the officer he was okay.

Paige's brown eyes flashed, catching the red and blue reflection from the vehicle's emergency lights outside.

Sergeant Peders questioned Brooks and the girls, his portable recorder taking down every word. "From your description, I know exactly where they've taken those horses," he said to Brooks. "We'll have something on them now. I'm almost sure of it. And, one way or another, we'll get the horses back, too."

"Back?" Meggie asked.

"Back on the range where they belong," he said to them.

A small crowd had gathered outside when Trevor and Soryn burst in.

"What's goin' on?" Trevor skidded in like a jet landing on a dirt strip. "Hey, aren't you the missing Dude?"

Brooks nodded. "Not anymore."

"Ah, you're the young man the sheriff talked with a few days ago, aren't you?" the sergeant said to Trevor.

"Yeah. It was me. And my cousin, Soryn here," he replied, turning to Soryn who stared at the bedraggled teenager standing in front of her. "That's him. So, hey, what's happening?"

"As soon as I finish getting the information I need, they can tell you themselves," Sergeant Peders said. "But first, you need to call your family, don't you Brooks?"

He shrugged. "Naw. It won't matter."

"Excuse me?" Paige turned to him, tossing the short, dark hair out of her wide, questioning eyes.

He turned to Paige, then the officer, a slow flush rising up his neck. "I don't really have a family." He paused, groping for the right words. "Uh, my folks were killed in a car accident a long time ago, so I just sort of drift from place to place. I thought the summer job and free bunkhouse at the Merk's ranch was a pretty cool deal. Guess I was dead rat wrong, huh?"

Paige swallowed hard. *No family? Just lives from place to place? That's terrible.*

"Of course I have to take you down to the station," the sergeant said.

"He can stay with us," Trevor put in quickly, giving Brooks a nod.

Paige felt a sudden rush of relief. "Cool. That will be a lot better than staying in jail or whatever."

Sergeant Peders hesitated, and then agreed it might be okay once they checked everything out. "First, you'll have to come with me. We'll need your help clearing a few hurdles, Brooks, including some background checks and a bit more information about you. If it all goes like I think it will and we get the evidence we need, then we'll want you to

99

testify in a court of law."

"Yeah, sure," Brooks said.

"But first I have to radio dispatch, then get in touch with the Local Brand Inspector and some other agencies so that we can get the Merk boys and those horses before it's too late." He reached for the phone clipped to his belt and walked to the back of the store.

Trevor hit the phone on the counter like a speeding bullet and by the time the officer was ready to leave, he had permission for Brooks to stay with his family. Sergeant Peders spoke with Trevor's parents for a few moments, telling them they were going to have to do some background checks and assessment before he left their jurisdiction. "Okay, do you need a ride?" he hung up the phone and turned to the kids.

Paige hesitated. "Do you have time? I mean, don't you have more important things to do?"

"Young lady," he replied, "The five of you are important. And just remember, I won't forget to notify the right people about that orphan colt. They'll know what to do."

"Okay, thank you, sir. Since Soryn and I were just closing up at the horse museum, maybe you could take us down to my house in Gold Hill?" Trevor suggested, glancing out at the impressive flashing lights on the vehicle. "We can all go our separate ways from there."

"Sure," the sergeant replied, clearing a path through the curious crowd to the waiting vehicle.

"Thanks!" Paige called back, leaving the bookstore and waving.

"Who are you waving to?" Meggie whispered. "Mark Twain or the lady with the broom?"

"Both of them," Paige snorted, brushing past her best friend and climbing into the back. "They're both very nice people."

Meggie frowned and climbed in beside her and Soryn.

"If you wouldn't mind, sir," Trevor buckled up next to Brooks who was sitting beside the sheriff, "could you leave the flashing lights on?"

"And also turn on the siren?" Paige added.

"Paige…" Meggie gave her a quick jab in the ribs.

Sergeant Peders explained why that wasn't done as he escorted them down the grade to the Gold Hill Hotel, just minutes away. They said goodbye to Brooks and promised to get back together as soon as everything got cleared up.

"Why did you ask him to turn on the lights and sirens?" Meggie asked Paige and Trevor the minute the officer was gone and they were standing in front of the hotel.

"Wouldn't you enjoy it?" Paige asked.

"No, I'd be embarrassed," Meggie replied. "People staring all the way from Virginia City to Gold Hill."

"What people? I only saw a few ground squirrels and a couple of cows." Trevor laughed.

"Okay, okay, it doesn't matter," Soryn said, walking between them waving her outstretched arms. "I want to hear more about how you found Brooks," she said, turning to Meggie and Paige. "Tell us everything. Was Brooks the guy you told us about? Was he the suspicious cowboy hanging out on those hills?"

Paige and Meggie tried to explain as much as they could, but the next day after the sheriff had cleared Brooks, he got to tell them himself.

Brooks took off his ratty cowboy hat and grinned, sitting down on some planks near the Yellow Jacket Mine. "Where to start, huh?"

Trevor sat down beside him. "Let's start with the part where they tied you up and left you to die in that mine."

Brooks nodded and began to tell his story again.

Paige brushed some dirt and mouse turds off a plank where she planned to sit down, when suddenly she saw movement behind the headframe of the mine. She jerked around, nearly losing her balance. "Oh my gosh! It's the colt!" she cried, pointing on the horizon. "Look!"

Meggie shaded her eyes against the bright afternoon sun and stared across the hills. "Little Beans. I can't believe it!"

Brooks rammed his hat back on his head. "Let's go!" he cried, leaping up. His feet hit the gravel, his shoulders lurched.

Brooks led the way up past the Yellow Jacket Mine toward the silhouette of the colt moving over the hill.

"Are you sure we shouldn't go back and report him first?" Meggie held back.

"No," he said, moving on. "Stay with me or go back yourselves. I can't lose him now!"

"Lose what?" Meggie asked. "You mean the colt?"

He didn't answer and Paige wondered if it was because he had a special understanding—a special feeling for the colt. Was it because they were both orphans?

"It's just gonna keep running, Paige!" Meggie called to her. "Do you really think we're going to catch him? Why are we doing this again? I think we're scaring the poor little thing!"

"Don't worry about the colt," Trevor said.

They paused.

"What?" Paige skidded to a halt.

"The colt won't leave the range."

"How do you know that?" Paige felt her throat tighten. "Have you seen it before?"

Trevor nodded.

"Well hey, why didn't you tell us?" Meggie asked.

Trevor threw up his hands and shrugged, adjusting his cap to keep the glare of the late afternoon sun from his eyes. "You'd never understand."

Won't ever leave the range? Paige wondered what he meant.

Brooks held his gaze, then turned again and continued following the colt, watching him disappear over the rise.

They left the trail finally, circling rugged crags of rock jutting up like witch fingers. It was almost as though the misshapen rocks were trying to hide the secrets of the hills and canyons. *But what secrets are they trying to hide?* Paige wondered. *Something else is going on, isn't it?* She had a strange kind of feeling inside her. It was almost as though this little colt was leading them to places they had to go. Part of her felt like they needed to leave it alone, but the other part of her knew they had to go on. *Why?* she wondered. *What's pulling me? Pulling Brooks?*

Finally they reached the ridge.

"A cemetery!" Meggie cried. "A little rundown cemetery in the middle of nowhere!" A metal gate hung loose, swinging in the wind.

"Yeah, and there he is," Brooks said, pointing. "There's the colt and he's circling the tombstone."

What tombstone? There's a whole bunch of tombstones. Paige grabbed Meggie's arm and stared at the colt. Her hand shook. *What's going on? Why are you circling that grave, Little Beans? What are you doing down there?*

The colt lurched when he saw them. Arched neck silhouetted against the setting sun, the small, elegant creature stood up on his haunches, then bolted.

"Let him run!" Trevor said, holding out his arms and motioning

103

them back. "Just let him run!"

Paige felt her heart back up in her throat. *Was Trevor right? Oh, Little Beans. Where are you going?* She watched the colt dart through the open gate, then gallop over the crest of the hill toward the setting sun.

"Okay. Okay now, follow me," Trevor went on, leading the way across the sand and rock toward the small, fenced enclosure where tombstones rose out of the ground like eerie desert flowers. Trevor paused by the gate hanging loose in the wind, then reached in his pocket and dropped some coins in a drop-box. "Sometimes the Comstock Cemetery people have to replace stolen headstones, or fix fences," he said to them. "It helps."

"You've been here before, then?" Meggie asked, fishing in her cutoffs for some coins. She found some quarters and dropped a few in the metal box.

He nodded. "I'm not the only one who comes to the grave," he told her, walking toward the tombstone surrounded by four white posts and an iron rope.

"The grave?" It was Meggie now.

"What's going on? Isn't this the grave we saw Little Beans circling?" Paige said, her interest growing, the pull getting stronger.

Soryn nodded. "Little Beans isn't the only one who comes here. They say people have been coming to this grave for over a hundred years."

Meggie walked up to the fenced tombstone where wilted flowers and old toys lay scattered and forgotten. "What's going on? Who's buried here?" She drew closer, straining to read the words on the cold white stone.

"Two boys," Trevor told them. "There was a bad snowstorm one Christmas Eve back in 1871. They went out to find their horse."

"So? What happened?" Paige stared at the grave, then threw her hand over her mouth. "Oh, no!" she cried. *They didn't come back, did they? This is so sad I don't like stories without happy endings.* She wanted to turn and run. *What're we doing here?* She turned away quickly and saw Brooks backing away from all of them. *He's feeling it, too, isn't he?*

"This is terrible!" Meggie said, gripping the fence and leaning closer so that she could read the words.

"In Affectionate Remembrance of Henry T. & John J. Jones…"

"…Who departed this life December 24th 1871," Brooks said from behind, his moist gray eyes welling up, "the beloved sons of Rob and Jane Jones. Henry T. age 14 years and John J. age 9 years and 9 months." His voice broke and he turned away.

Everyone turned and stared at Brooks.

He knows. But how can he? He can't be reading the words from that far back. What's going on? Paige bit her lip, tried to think straight. *How can he know?*

Meggie turned back to the tombstone and continued on:

"They are not dead but gone before, our precious darling boys, Death wrapped them in a snowy shroud to awake 'mid Heavenly joys. Their horse stood over them with care, by the hand of God was holden there, Three days and nights on the mountain lay, Guarded by Angels until bourne away."

Tears zigzagged down her cheeks and she turned away.

Brooks walked past them all and knelt down, taking off his favorite leather hat. He lay it down in the hapless collection of toys and dried flowers. "It's not much, but it's all I've got."

"Brooks?" Paige said with unsteady words. "Brooks—wha…?"

"Brooks Henry Jones," he replied, getting up. Moist eyes caught the reflection of the red sun, but he didn't care. "I've searched all my life for this place."

"Wait a minute." It was Meggie now. "You—you said you always wanted to come to Nevada, didn't you? So—is this why?"

Brooks nodded, his watery eyes still catching the sun's reflection. "After my folks were gone, I found some pictures. One of them was a picture of this tombstone–except the tombstone looked different." He pulled the faded photograph out of his back pocket, showing them all.

Everyone fell speechless.

"The original tombstone was stolen," Trevor gathered up his words and spoke finally. "The Comstock cemetery people replaced it."

Brooks nodded with understanding. "The words were the same. I knew those words by heart because my grandfather used to tell me the story of his great grandfather's brothers and how I was named after one of the boys." His voice caught. "I always wanted to come to this place, especially after my grandfather died and there was nobody left. I knew that they were buried somewhere around here, but I didn't know how I'd find it."

"And the horse brought you here, didn't he?" Paige felt the catch in her voice.

"Yeah, he did," Brooks said.

Trevor walked up and stood beside Brooks. "I knew you were looking for something. I mean those binoculars and all. I just never figured…"

Brooks nodded, then turned and watched the colt disappear over the crest of the hill.

"Run, Little Beans!" Paige cried out, waving in the wind.

Brooks squared his shoulders and smiled on the horizon of a new day. "Thanks, little mustang," he said quietly, "You're not alone. And neither am I."

Brooks Henry Jones squared his shoulders and smiled on the horizon of a new day. He walked away from the grave with his new friends, but his old leather hat would stay and remember.

JONES BOYS TOMBSTONE, COMSTOCK CEMETERY

⌒ Jumbo Springs ⌒

Trevor, Soryn, and Brooks hiked up the gravel road to say goodbye to Meggie and Paige.

"They rescued the horses," Trevor spoke first, grinning from ear to ear. "They're making sure they're not injured and then they'll be setting them free."

"Yesss!" Paige and Meggie gave two thumbs up. "Whoa and YES!"

"The Merk brothers don't get off so easy, though," Soryn added. "Guess they trade their ranch for an iron corral."

"And I'm probably stayin' on with Trevor and his folks," Brooks told them. "After legal stuff gets cleared up, I might even have a job with an agency that helps protect the wild horses. I'm looking into that right now."

"Until then you can help my aunt and me at the museum," Soryn added. "That is if you don't mind hanging out in a boxcar for awhile."

Paige felt so good inside. "Brooks, that is too cool! I am really glad about how things turned out for you."

Brooks nodded and gave her and Meggie a slow half-smile. "Yeah, me too. And thanks for risking so much and going into that mine and saving my life. It could have been a ghost or a…"

"A Tommyknocker," Meggie put in. "And, you're welcome."

"Hey, I've been meaning to ask. What's a Tommyknocker anyway?" Paige turned to Trevor. "I think they were with me down in the mine. Maybe they were taking care of me? You said you knew what they were."

"They're rats," Trevor told them.

"Rats?" Paige spit out the word, trying to keep from having heart failure right there on the spot. She grimaced, knotting her fists. *Oh, eesh, I can't believe it was actually rats making all those terrible little crunching noises. Crawling all over in there.* "This is too disgusting."

"Yeah. The legend I like best says that Tommyknockers were just rats. When the miners had their little beady-eyed buddies around eating and crunching their pasties, they knew they were safe."

Pasties? How about my chocolate chip cookies? Memories of her lunch spilling through the slats in the mine where she had fallen returned suddenly. *Rats? How gross.* "This is too disgusting and I'm not sure I believe your version of the legend anyway," she said to Trevor. "Tommyknockers were the Cornish miners' little people, not rats."

"Who knows?" Trevor shrugged and went on. "What we know for sure is that creatures *know* when there's gonna be danger. A cave-in. Fire. Whatever. They know."

Soryn nodded in agreement, sitting down on a stump beside the camp table. "I don't know how it happens, but sometimes animals—creatures—know and feel things we can't."

"Like the horse that stayed by those boys until somebody came," Meggie said.

"And Little Beans who stayed by me when I was trapped in that mineshaft," Paige added.

"Yeah, even me," Brooks said, turning toward the hills where the horses still ran free. "Things just sort of have a way of working out."

"It's the Law," Paige said.

"Huh?" Brooks stared down at his new friend.

"Ghostowner's Law."

They laughed, then turned toward the hills. A herd of mustangs came galloping over the ridge, manes and tails flying in the hot summer wind. "Oh!" Paige threw her hand over her mouth, holding back the sudden rush of happiness. And tears. "I see him. Look, Meggie! Little Beans!"

Meggie grabbed Paige's arm. "Paige…he—he's…"

"I know," Paige said through her tears. "He's out in front!"

"Run, little mustang!" Brooks Henry Jones called out, waving. "Run like you were born to do!"

"Be free."

"Let 'em Run"

110

ENDNOTES

Historical Facts:

The Jones boys' gravesite is located in the Comstock Cemetery near Gold Hill, Nevada. Original headstone was replaced by the cemetery association after it was stolen.

For over 100 years, people have been bringing flowers and toys to the grave.

Archives and local records contain small pieces of historical data on the Jones boys.

Chollar Mine: Established in 1861. Still holding mine tours to this day.

Legends of the Tommyknockers still exist.

Gold Hill history.

Virginia City history.

Virginia & Truckee Railroad still operates for tourists.

1998 wild horse massacre

Let 'em Run Foundation continues to work for the preservation of the wild horses.

"HISTORY," someone said, "BELONGS TO THOSE WHO WRITE IT."

John and Henry Jones deserve to be remembered.